July
Is Coming

Sandra
Waggoner

Sable
CREEK
PRESS

Cover and text design by Diane King, dkingdesigner.com
Cover photos: © And19sv | Dreamstime.com - Diamond Ring On A Shoelace Photo; © Neillockhart | Dreamstime.com - Old Shack Sun Beams Photo

Scripture taken from the King James Version. Public domain.

Published by Sable Creek Press, Glendale, Arizona
sablecreekpress.com

Library of Congress Control Number: 2014952655

ISBN 978-0-98906675-4

Printed in the United States of America.

THIS book is dedicated especially to all wayward sheep who feel they have done something so terrible God does not want them or love them anymore. Just so you know ... God still loves you so much that he is watching and waiting for you. Please, please come home.

"And he arose, and came to his father. But when he was yet a great way off, his father saw him, and had compassion, and ran, and fell on his neck, and kissed him." Luke 15:20

OTHER BOOKS BY SANDRA WAGGONER

DANGER AT WOLF ROCK

SON OF AN HONEST MAN

GATLIN FIELDS SERIES:
MAGGIE'S TREASURE
IN THE SHADOW OF THE ENEMY
WHEN SECRETS COME HOME
AFTER THE DUST SETTLES

CONTENTS

The Dragon

THE train whistle blew and scattered a bunch of cattle off the tracks. July smiled as she watched them run. They weren't supposed to be there, but they must have busted through the barbed wire fence somewhere. A calf bawled and chased her long-horned mama.

July wanted to giggle. She stole a glance at Mrs. Drunyon in the seat beside her. Mrs. Drunyon stared straight ahead. Her mouth etched a grim line across her face, and a few hairs dared straggle from the bobby pins holding tight the bun at the back of her neck. The only thing moving was the orange flower on her hat. It swayed in time with the roll of the train.

July figured life hadn't been easy on the older woman. The kids at the orphanage said her husband had gone stark-raving mad. Long before this Great Depression had started, he had pilfered money from the bank where he worked. Then when everything was gone, he hanged himself. Mrs. Drunyon had found him the next morning in the shed. He had left a note stuck under the windshield wiper of their shiny black Model-T explaining that everything was lost. Even the money he had stolen from the bank was gone—or at least never found.

Sandra Waggoner

Mrs. Drunyon had run crazy down Main Street until her son had caught her and calmed her down enough to find out what was wrong. Mr. Drunyon had been right. Everything had been lost, and Mrs. Drunyon was lucky to find a job teaching at the orphanage half-way across the state. No one close to the scene of Mr. Drunyon's crime and suicide would hire his wife. She had been at the orphanage for a few years, and only whispers informed July of the ugly truth. Most of the kids called Mrs. Drunyon "The Dragon," but not when she was in hearing distance. Someone said The Dragon had volunteered for the job of taking July to her grandparents' town because it was in the very place she and Mr. Drunyon had lived—and where the tragedy had taken place. She wondered if her grandparents knew The Dragon.

Grandparents. Her heart thudded almost to a standstill. She remembered Mama looking into her eyes, swiping a tear from her own cheek and whispering that July's eyes were the same beautiful deep blue as her grandpa's. Mama had spoken with such love that July had begged Mama to take her to grandpa's house. Mama had looked off into the distance. "It can never be, July. I cannot disgrace them. They must never know."

"Know what?" July had asked, but mama was a closed book. July never found what Mama had done, and now she wasn't sure she wanted to meet her mama's parents, much less live with them.

July sighed. She had tried to sleep, but her stomach was knotted. A million questions raced through her mind. What if her grandparents didn't want her? What if she didn't like them? How could she like them if they didn't like her mama? What if they expected her to be perfect? With that thought, July made an attempt to smooth down the short, dark hair that sprayed wherever it wanted to go. What if her grandparents didn't like short hair? Mama said short hair was easier to keep. It didn't take as much water and soap to wash it, and they only had the broken half of an old comb. It had grown some since she had been at the orphanage, but not a lot. She closed her blue eyes to calm the "what if's," and if it were possible, to forget them.

July rested against her seat. She pulled out the thick gold band hanging on a well-worn shoelace about her neck and held it so it would catch the sunshine. A gold band circled the single, huge diamond. The stone reflected pastel glitter drops so that they scattered and splashed all about her. She loved watching the sparkles dance. Her mama had treasured this ring. July felt a tear wishing to slide over her cheek as her thoughts settled on Mama. She blinked to hold the tear back. Crying would not make the lonesome hurt go away. Life had been rough for Mama, but July always knew her mama loved her. From the time she was little, Mama would hold her and rock her and sing sweet lullabies to her. At the end, July had held Mama, rocked her and sang the same sweet songs. Then Mama had pressed this very ring into her hand with the words, "Never forget I will love you to the end of time." Mama had closed her gray-blue eyes to never open them again, and July had kissed Mama's soft cheek. That's when July knew endings were not always happy.

"And where did you get that, young lady?" Mrs. Drunyon gaped. "My word, it looks like gold and a real diamond. Why, it looks like … " Mrs. Drunyon gasped and never finished the sentence.

July's heart jumped, and in a flash, she shoved the ring back inside her blouse.

Mrs. Drunyon pushed her head closer to July. She clicked out the words, "I asked you a question, young lady. Where did you get that ring?"

"It was my mama's, ma'am," said July.

"Really? Your mother owned that expensive piece of jewelry and lived in squalor? I don't think you are telling me the truth." She narrowed her eyes, and July watched them spark with an idea.

"Well, you might as well hand it over because all property of value is to be confiscated to help pay the orphanage for your outstanding debt." Mrs. Drunyon held out her hand demanding the ring.

Now July knew why they called this woman The Dragon. The girl tensed with determination. "No." She would not give up this ring, this one link she had left to her mama.

The Dragon gasped, almost spurting fire. "You'll not refuse an order from me, young lady. Hand over the ring."

"No, ma'am." July's hand was shaking as she placed it over the spot where the ring fell at her neck. "This is the only thing I have left from my mama, and I won't give it to you."

The woman grabbed July's hand and ripped it away from her chest.

In horror, July twisted and jumped up, tumbling with the roll of the train. She fell over Mrs. Drunyon's legs, scrambled across her lap and landed on the floor. Crawling to keep her balance, July smashed her head into the legs of the train conductor.

"Whoa there, young'un … uh … missy, let me help you." He pulled July to her feet.

With wild eyes the girl searched the aisle. The Dragon's breath was hot on July's neck.

Mrs. Drunyon patted her hat and smiled at the conductor. "Thank you, sir. As you know, I'm seeing the pitiful orphan to her grandparents in Plevna, Kansas. Her background is a bit shady, so I should not be surprised she stole my gold wedding band. She has it strung around her neck, and I wonder if you would be so kind as to help me retrieve it?"

"A thief," someone breathed.

July's mouth dropped wide. "That's a lie!" she shouted.

"You can see how rude she is, can't you, sir? She talked to all of the adults at the orphanage in this very manner." The Dragon's eyes held an evil sparkle.

The conductor dropped his hold on July. "Uh, ma'am," he began. July thought he was a bit scared of The Dragon, too. Yet, she could feel the doubt in his voice and was afraid he believed the woman. The conductor took a step away from Mrs. Drunyon, and that was July's chance. She skidded around him and bolted for the door.

"Stop her! She's a thief! Someone stop her!" Mrs. Drunyon yelled.

Passengers swiveled in their seats. Some half stood, some gaped, but all watched.

"Don't just sit there!" Mrs. Drunyon screeched, "Someone stop that thief!"

"Don't open that door, missy." The conductor said as he bobbed his head from July back to Mrs. Drunyon.

"Ma'am, I would feel better if you had the station manager search this girl. It would be more of his job description, not mine." He patted his pocket. "I got my rule book here, and I pretty well have it memorized. I could get into big trouble and lose my job, and jobs are mighty hard to come by. President Hoover isn't getting this Depression undepressed fast enough for me."

So just July could see, the conductor gave a slight wink, and July thought he kept talking to give her more time to get away and to cool The Dragon down. It didn't work. The Dragon had turned fire red.

"Sir, all you have to do is hold the girl. I will snatch the ring." Mrs. Drunyon tried to step around the conductor, bumping into seats and passengers as she fought to keep her balance with the sway of the train. Then with a mighty shove, she pushed him aside and marched toward the frantic girl.

July smashed her shoulder against the heavy door as hard as she could. It would not budge. She kicked and pounded it, but The Dragon was like a huge bird of prey. She clutched ahold of July's arm and swung her about. The terrified girl kicked the woman in the leg. The Dragon cried out, lost her death grip and with the swerve of the train was knocked to the floor. July jumped over the crumpled orphanage woman and scrambled towards the door at the other end of the passenger car.

"Whoa, there, missy. I can't let you go out a door whilst this train is moving. You might fall under the train, and those wheels would cut you to shreds. Please. Hold on a minute." The conductor wiped sweat from his brow.

July took a step away. She was caught between him and The Dragon. She studied the conductor's face. He looked honest. She patted the spot where the ring hung. "Mr. Conductor, this is my mama's wedding ring. I'm not going to let that woman take it from me. This is all I have left. If you try to make me give it to her, I'll jump from the train."

The conductor shook his head. "It's not my job to take things from passengers, missy. I promise I won't. However, I want you to know that when we stop at the station, it could become a police matter. It's their job. I'm sorry." The man tipped his head to the side and raised his shoulders showing that was the way of things, and he couldn't do anything to change it. Passengers gasped as The Dragon grabbed an old man's cane and lunged at the girl.

July tumbled across an empty seat, hitting a gentleman and sending his newspaper flying past the conductor. "Sorry, mister," she called back, struggling to keep her balance as she hurried down the aisle.

July reached the back door of the passenger car and frantically worked the handle until it gave way. She surged out the door and grasped the platform rail. She felt sick as she saw the earth rushing by beneath her. The sound of loud voices was getting closer.

"Ma'am, you're not going to follow that poor child out there. You'll force her to jump," the conductor called.

"I don't care if she does jump, as long as I get that ring first. Now, let me go," The Dragon sneered. "This is none of your business."

"Lady, it should be the business of everyone on this train." A new and deeper voice joined them. "I'll not stand by and watch a defenseless child get killed."

July's knuckles were white as she gripped the rail to keep from falling. She turned her head from the sight of the ground streaking by below. She peeked through the door to get a good look at the man behind that voice. He was the gentleman with the newspaper—the one she had jumped over earlier when she charged down the aisle to get away from The Dragon.

"Defenseless? Don't you kid yourself. That child is far from defenseless." July heard The Dragon's shaky, high-pitched voice.

"Lady, I'll not let you take matters into your own hands." The man stood blocking the way of The Dragon.

"Thank you, sir. I'll take it from here," the conductor said. The train whistle blew as the train began slowing down. "This will be the Plevna station and the stop where this woman and child get off. I'll escort them to the station master, and he can turn the matter over to the police."

The gentleman filled the aisle between the woman and the little girl and turned to appeal to the conductor. "Look, why don't you take this lady, and let me persuade the little girl."

The conductor nodded and motioned to Mrs. Drunyon. "Please, Ma'am."

"You've not heard the end of this." Mrs. Drunyon pointed a bony finger at the two men, then waved it at the passengers of the car threatening all of them.

July watched as the conductor took Mrs. Drunyon's arm and escorted her toward the door at the opposite end of the passenger car. Then she studied the kind man slowly heading her way. July looked at the ground passing beneath her. The train wasn't going as fast now. She might be able to jump without being hurt too badly. She stepped onto the lowest rail, and with hopeless eyes begging for understanding, she looked to the man easing closer.

"Please, little one? Please, come down?" he pleaded.

She dropped her gaze to the ground. She could feel the heat from the train's wheels, and their whine was deafening, but she might have a chance. She placed her foot on the next rail and touched the place where her mama's ring hung beneath her blouse. The wind ripped at her hair and billowed her skirts. She let go and stood tall, taking one final glance at the man.

"Oh, dear Lord, no," the man cried out as he dove toward the helpless little girl.

Deal

WRAPPED safely in the man's strong arms, July felt the wild, hungry wind claim her being. Then they hit the ground hard, rolling over and over again. When finally they stopped, the man heaved great gasps of air as his arms slacked his hold on her. She pulled away and watched while he struggled to turn himself to lean on one arm.

"Mister, are you okay?" July asked.

The man didn't even try to talk. He just nodded his head. July didn't think he was telling the truth. "You sure? Do you think you are going to die?"

"No, I'm not going to die. I think I'm fine, but tomorrow may tell a different story. Are you okay?"

July smiled. "Yep, Mister, you make a pretty soft landing."

The man chuckled. "I'll bet I do. I'll tell my wife I need to keep those few extra pounds I carry around just for things like this. Better yet, I'll have you tell her."

This time July laughed.

The man sobered. "What are you going to do now?"

July looked to the horizon and shrugged her shoulders.

"From what I overheard on the train, I take it you have grand-parents in Plevna?"

July studied him. "Yep, I do."

"Then I'm sure they will help you."

July never let her eyes leave his. "I hope they will. I've never met them before. I don't think they helped my mama much."

"I see," said the man.

July could tell he didn't know what to do with her. She knew how to make that easy for him. "Look, I don't know who you are, but I'm not your responsibility. Thanks for helping me not get killed jumping off the train, but I can take care of myself now." She brushed off her skirt and stood to leave.

"Wait a minute, young lady. I just stepped into this mystery, and I'm not leaving until I get it solved. Now, let me introduce myself. My name is Sam Bryan, and you might be needing me. I am the only lawyer in Plevna, Kansas and the surrounding area."

July took a step back, "I didn't steal this ring from Mrs. Drun-yon, Mr. Sam Bryan. It was my mama's ring, and I intend to keep it."

"Yes, I can see that." He turned on his hands and knees to crawl to a standing position, then straightened his suit coat. "First, let me tell you that I believe it was your mama's ring, and I believe you will keep it. It would be much better to have the law on your side, though. I'd like to help you. Do you think you can trust me?"

July squinted, looking him up and down. Finally she nodded, spit in her hand, and swiped it down the side of her dress. Then she held out her hand for the lawyer to shake. "Sorry I had to wipe the spit-seal off, but my mama made me promise not to use the seal on grown-ups."

Humor lit his eyes, but he smothered any chuckle that might have tried to escape. He stretched his hand to hers and shook. "Deal. Now, you come with me, and we'll face this crowd together."

In the distance July could see the train had stopped at the station. She also saw a crowd of people that seemed to be looking her way. She felt her heart pounding all over again. She didn't know her grandma and grandpa. What if they tried to make her give the ring back? What if the police tried? What if everyone believed Mrs. Drunyon? That was what usually happened. People tended to believe the adults over children. What if they believed she stole the ring? What if she got sent to a reform school for girls? She had been threatened with reform school while she was at the orphanage. All the kids had been threatened at one time or another. It was like a dark cloud hanging over her. She was only ten years old, but she knew if she went to reform school it would follow her the rest of her life.

Sam Bryan gently held his hand to her. "It will be alright, I promise."

July had that feeling again like when she jumped from the train. Her eyes gathered a distant, defeated look, and she wished she could just be swept away.

Sam Bryan stepped closer and took her hand gently into his. "I don't even know you. What is your name?"

She smiled and beamed up at him as his question pulled her back to the present. "Sir, I am June July, but my mama called me July on account her name was May June Calendar, but her mama called her June because her mama's name was May. My mama said my grandma thought it would be special to have calendar names since she married a man named Calendar. So we are May, June and July. Better yet, we are May, May June, and June July."

"Slow down the train, Miss June July Calendar. That is enough to confuse even a lawyer," he laughed. "But let me tell you right now, I think God smiled upon you."

They had begun walking toward the station. July stopped, pulled her hand from his and crossed her arms, "Really? I'm not sure about this God smiling thing. I've talked to him, and we don't see eye-to-eye on things."

"Oh? What things?"

"Well, I told him I needed my daddy to come back. And what was God's answer? Well, it seems no one even knows if my daddy is alive or dead." She held up her first finger. "That's number one. Number two," she put up her next finger. "I told him I needed my mama, but you can see God didn't think so. She died. And, number three, I really talked to God about the orphanage thing, but I was stuck there for almost six months. That was three, and anyone knows that it is one, two, three strikes and you're out. But I tried again. Number four." She held up four fingers and shoved them toward the lawyer. "And look at now. After this I might be facing reform school after all. If God is really up there somewhere, he isn't listening to me at all." July was on the stormy side of serious.

Sam Bryan didn't dare smile. "I see," he paused in thought. "Maybe you don't know God well enough, or better yet, maybe we could learn how to *ask* God for miracles instead of *telling* him we need them."

She tipped her head and squinted, "You think I don't know God?" She stopped and wiped her hand over her face. "I s'pose that could be. I guess he's somewhere up there in heaven. I just thought he knew me and he would listen to me. I didn't know there was a certain way to ask him for miracles." She stopped and glared at the lawyer. "If you tell me these things about God and miracles, does it cost more than me keeping my mama's ring?"

Sam Bryan smiled, "Just for you, June July Calendar, there is no charge on any of the above."

"Honest? Not even the ring part?"

"Honest." The lawyer laughed this time.

July spit in her hand, swiped it down her side and stretched it to the lawyer for the second time. He shook her hand by placing both of his over her right hand and then held on with his left and turned to walk toward the growing crowd at the station.

"Mr. Bryan, I don't usually let anyone know when I'm scared, but my heart is going faster than the train we just jumped off of ever did, even going down the steepest hill."

"Stay with me, Miss June July Calendar, and I'll keep you safe."

She looked up at him. "Are you kind of like a daddy?"

His eyebrows rose. "Yes, I believe I am. All daddies should be very protective of their little girls."

"I sure wish I had my daddy." She looked toward the sky. "Please?" She turned to the lawyer. "Does *please* help when you talk to God?"

"I'm sure it does," he smiled. "Now, listen to me. I rather think you are used to taking matters in your own hands, but I want you to let me do the talking. Do not say a thing unless I ask you to. Understand?"

July nodded. "Yes, sir."

"Good, because we are about there, and I see the station manager and the police and your Mrs. Drunyon." He scanned the crowd.

"She's not *my* Mrs. Drunyon. Back at the orphanage we called her The Dragon."

Sam Bryan laughed heartily. "That may be, and it may fit her very well, but do not call her that here and now. Am I clear? I believe it would hurt our case."

"Yes, sir," she said.

"Great. Now, take a deep breath because we will face your dragon along with the rest of the opposition shortly."

"Not *my* dragon," she whispered from clenched teeth and peeked up to Mr. Bryan to see if he had heard. He was smiling. July shrugged her shoulders. She wasn't sure what he meant about opposition, but she sure needed a deep breath. One hand was safe in the lawyer's hand. Quickly she put her other hand over the front of her blouse to feel her mama's ring. Maybe it would give her the courage she needed to face The Dragon. Again she turned her eyes to heaven and mouthed the words, "I'm asking *please* this time, God. Please help Mr. Bryan and me keep my mama's ring and not go to reform school. *Please.*"

God Smiled

THE Dragon pointed her finger like a monstrous claw. "That's the little brat of a thief!" she shrieked. "She's the one who stole my ring!"

A policeman tried to keep up with her and calm her down at the same time. "Ma'am, just stand back, and we'll take care of the situation."

July slid closer to Mr. Bryan and took a tighter grip on his hand. She looked up at him. "Are you sure you can handle this?"

"I'll have it under control in a jiffy," he nodded. "You just keep quiet and follow my lead."

"Yes, sir."

The lawyer held onto July's hand as he strode forward to meet the policeman. "Pete, I'm glad to see you," Mr. Bryan smiled. "I'd like you to meet my friend and client, Miss June July Calendar. July, this is Mr. Pete Crosby. I have helped him in many cases. In fact, I've known him since he was knee-high to a grasshopper, and I helped him through the police academy. Right now we're working on Pete becoming the new sheriff because our old one is retiring. You two go ahead and shake."

July felt a little more comfortable as she stretched out her hand. She didn't spit on it this time because there was no bargain to seal.

Pete cleared his throat and hesitated. Nevertheless his smile was warm as he took July's hand. "Glad to meet you, Miss July." When he dropped her hand he turned again to the lawyer. "Sam, we have a problem here." He swung his hand toward Mrs. Drunyon, "This lady says the little one stole her wedding ring."

Mrs. Drunyon nosed closer. "You better believe she stole my ring, and I can tell you where she put it." The Dragon glared.

July couldn't help checking to make sure the ring was still safely under her blouse where she had placed it.

The Dragon didn't miss the gesture. "Right there," she pointed. "See, she put her hand over the place she hid it."

Sam Bryan stepped in front of July and stuck his hand out to shake with The Dragon. "And you are?"

"Mrs. Helen Drunyon, if it's any of your business. I am in charge of this thief, and I will take charge of her now. I intend to see that she gets into a reform school where they will teach her how to behave. Now, if you will step aside, sir."

Mr. Bryan did not back away from July or The Dragon. "Mrs. Drunyon, I am a lawyer and … "

"Good!" the Dragon's eyes lit up. "I may need your services. The orphanage will pay quite well."

Sparkles danced in the lawyer's eyes. "I'm sorry, Mrs. Drunyon. I couldn't. It would be a conflict of interest."

"What?" she frowned.

"I've taken Miss June July Calendar's case. I believe she claims the ring as hers since it belonged to her late mother."

The crowd rippled with laughter.

The Dragon's mouth gaped wide. "How dare you! The orphanage will have that ring, and I will see to it." She reached around to grab July.

"Wait a moment, Mrs. Drunyon, I believe your job was to deliver the child to her grandparents? Her grandparents live right here in Plevna, Kansas?"

"Yes," The Dragon glared. "And I would appreciate your letting me do my job. Now, please give me the child."

Sam Bryan smiled. "Mrs. Drunyon, I can help. Her grandparents are right there. If you will excuse me, I shall be glad to introduce them."

The Dragon whipped about, and July watched as her bulging eyes fell on the couple and lit with recognition. "Are you sure you want the job? She stole my wedding ring."

The lawyer held up his hand as if he were stopping traffic. "Allegedly, stole the ring. I'm afraid you have no proof. That makes it your word against hers, Mrs. Drunyon."

"Hey," July burst from behind Mr. Bryan. "I don't know what *allegedly* means, but I didn't steal this ring. It was my mama's."

The lawyer held her hand firmly. "July, remember my instructions?"

"But I heard you," July hissed. "You said I stole the ring, and I did not steal the ring!"

"July, I said *allegedly*. That means to accuse with no proof. I also said you were to let me do the talking. Am I understood?" The lawyer didn't give an inch.

For a moment July was steaming. Finally, she tipped her head in agreement, but not without trying to have the last word. "Without proof, huh?" She watched the lawyer's eyes widen with warning. July took her empty hand, pretended to zip her lips closed and throw the key away.

"That's better."

Mrs. Drunyon smiled, and for the first time July thought maybe she wasn't as ancient and mean as it seemed. "That little snip will get under your skin," said Mrs. Drunyon. "She'll sure make your nerves go wild. I know how to work with her. I can take her off your hands and save you a lot of trouble."

July wanted to tell The Dragon that she could get under people's skin, too, but the girl checked Sam Bryan's face and decided against it. He was a shade of warning red, and he looked like he was choosing his words carefully. "Mrs. Drunyon, why don't you go ahead and let your orphanage lawyer handle this case."

She huffed. "You had better believe I will contact our lawyer." She turned and poked her bony finger at the couple waiting to claim July. "You have your job cut out for you, and mark my words, you're going to regret this day." With that she shoved her way through the crowd and out of July's sight.

July was so mad she wanted to cry. Then like sun breaking through storm clouds she laughed and hugged Mr. Sam Bryan. "We won the case, just like you promised. I have my ring. We won the case." July began to dance about him.

"Hold on there, child," he spoke softly. "I think we just won round number one."

July paused an instant. "So there are rounds?" She twisted her lips. "But I believe in you. If you knocked out round number one, you can knock out the next rounds, too."

The lawyer smiled. "You are a breath of sunshine, girl." He patted her hand. "Let's meet your grandparents." He looked over her shoulder to the couple holding hands. Gently, he turned July to face them, but she deliberately looked toward the distant horizon instead. "Mr. and Mrs. Calendar, this is June July Calendar."

Shyly, July pulled her eyes away from the sky to greet them. She didn't want to leave Sam Bryan. He was her new friend. Friends were comfortable and hard to come by.

The man who must be her grandpa carried a touch of a smile. Grandpas were expected to be old, but he didn't look as old as July had figured he would look. He had dark hair slightly touched with gray. He was clean shaven and tall. July thought his eyes were the bluest blue she had ever seen, and they seemed to hold a welcome for her. Mama had said July had those same eyes. A spark of warm pride kindled in her heart. The lady next to him took in a breath as her hand flew to her mouth. July heard her whisper. "Ezra. Ezra, she looks just like our June." Then she brushed a tear from her cheek.

The whole crowd hushed as if its heart was holding a beat.

July stared. This lady was the spitting image of July's mama with a few fine lines and a kiss of silver in her hair. Something inside made her want to run and throw her arms around this woman, but she wasn't Mama. She only looked like her mama. July hadn't cried since that last shovel of dirt had landed with a thud on Mama's grave. She refused to cry now, but her insides felt like they were bursting with a storm of tears.

The woman dropped to her knees with both hands to her face. There was more than a tear now. That lady was crying the cloud burst July was holding inside.

The man beside her knelt and tenderly patted his wife, all the while watching July. Slowly he rose and crossed to the little girl. He held out his hand to her and waited for her to take it. "July?"

She nodded because she couldn't trust her voice to answer.

"I believe I'm your grandpa, and we are so glad God has given you to us."

July was lost in his deep blue eyes.

"Would you like to come meet your grandma?" he asked.

July swallowed. Could she touch this woman that seemed as if she were so like her mama come from the grave?

Her grandpa felt the girl's hesitation. "She would love to meet you, and I know she didn't mean to cry. She is not sad or sorry. It isn't your fault she's crying. We didn't even know we had a June July until we got a notice in the mail a couple of weeks ago. And, July, I think you are your grandma's answer to hope."

Still, July felt glued to the spot.

"Please?" Grandpa pleaded.

July was drowning in his eyes. Quickly she turned to her lawyer friend. He simply tipped his head to give her courage and whispered so only those close could hear. "Child, God has truly smiled upon you."

July gave a faint nod to her grandpa and took hold of his hand.

It was only a couple of steps, but July dragged behind. When she was within reach, her grandma wrapped her arms around the little girl and pulled her so close to her shaking body July could feel her grandma's heart pounding. Then the storm July had been holding back broke loose. She cried. She cried because Grandma looked like Mama, but she wasn't. She cried because she would never feel Mama's arms around her again, and oh, how she wished she could.

One by one, the crowd tip-toed away from the heart-breaking scene. The lawyer was the last to leave. He rested his hand on Ezra's shoulder and made a promise: "Anything you need, Ezra, you just let me know."

The Mansion

JULY heard Grandpa clear his throat. "Ladies, why don't we head home? I still have chores, and we have the rest of time to get to know one another."

July pulled away from Grandma and looked up. She could tell Grandpa didn't mean anything badly. He just didn't know how to help girls not cry. She stood and waited for Grandpa to help Grandma up. July surveyed the area. There was an old Hudson and a couple of wagons. She had no idea which might be theirs, so she waited.

Prickles trickled over her skin when Grandpa took hold of one of her hands, and Grandma took the other. Could two people she had never met before really care about her? She snuck a peek first at Grandpa. He had his eyes planted ahead. Then she looked over at Grandma, who kept brushing tears from her cheeks. They passed the Hudson, so that must not be their auto. July began to wonder as they went by all the wagons. She guessed they must be walking. The quiet was beginning to bother July, and she had a lot of questions. "So we don't live very far from the train station?"

"Not too far," Grandpa said.

July thought of something else to ask. "What do you want me to call you?"

Again it was Grandpa who answered. "The twins call us Grams and Gramps. I reckon that would be the easiest."

"That means I have cousins?" July smiled. Surely cousins would be fun. The kids at the orphanage had been fun for the most part, so cousins should be even better. "Are they boys or girls?"

Gramps chuckled, "You got yourself one of each."

July skipped a step. "How old are they?" If Grams and Gramps hadn't been holding her hands she would have been crossing her fingers.

Grams answered this time. "Eleven. They turned eleven on May first."

"May Day. Oh, I like that. They are almost my age. There is only a year's difference, and that is about the same."

July noticed a quick exchange of glances between Grams and Gramps. That surely meant something, but she didn't know what. Then the thought hit like a bomb. What if they didn't live here? What if she never got to see them? She took a deep breath expecting the worst before she asked the next question. "Do they live close?"

"Right through the tree row, July. Right through the tree row," Gramps said.

July could tell something funny was going on. She continued to poke at the subject. "Will we get to play much?"

Immediately, she knew she hit on the sore part. Gramps looked straight ahead and cleared his throat, but he was not the one who answered.

"I hope so," Grams said.

July stopped walking and waited until they both faced her. "Why? What's wrong?"

Gramps's eyes sparkled. "Go on, May. You explain this one."

Grams raised her eyebrows at Gramps, and July was sure there was some secret passing between them. "Ezra?"

Gramps shook his head. "I wouldn't know how to begin ... nicely enough."

"July, honey. Sybil, their mother, has rather highfalutin' airs. You probably don't know what that means."

"Highfalutin' airs? You bet your bottom dollar I know what that means. It means uppity—thinking more of your ownself than those around you do."

Gramps heehawed. "Bright little thing, isn't she, May?"

Grams hid a smile behind her hand. "Well, yes. Yes, she is." She turned back to July. "I'd have to say you hit the nail on the head, my dear."

"Does that mean my Aunt Sybil has to approve of me before she will let me play with my cousins? Because if it does, I can be on my best behavior. I did it most all the time at the orphanage." July said.

Gramps studied his grandchild. "I believe you should be on your best behavior all the time, Miss July," he said wisely.

July's eyes twinkled. "Yes, sir."

Gramps groaned. "July, I forgot about your bags. I guess we had better mosey on back to the station and get them."

"Nope. There are no bags. The orphanage burned the clothes I came in and only let me keep this set," said July. "It's all I got."

Gramps rubbed his hand over his face. "May, we can get a few things from Celie. They are close to the same in age, and their size is almost the same. Or, you can pull out that box of flour sacks and sew."

"I'll ask Sybil, but I'll be glad to sew. It will be like old times."

July didn't know for sure what they were talking about, but her Grams seemed to glow.

Gramps stopped. "Well, July, my dear, this is it. We've had it in the family for years. I hope we can keep it in the family. Times are hard."

Sandra Waggoner

July stood in front. A tree row of tall cedars graced both sides of the house. About the wraparound porch, lilac bushes bloomed. July thought they must have a good well and do a bunch of bucket carrying because water was scarce. It was a small two-story clapboard building. It was in need of paint, with empty patches on the roof where a few shingles were missing. There were no screens on the windows, and in the light breeze, curtains billowed out of the open panes. A hand-painted sign was nailed next to the screen door. It read: Pastor and Mrs. Calendar. July's eyes grew wide, "You're a pastor?"

"Mmm, among other things. I pretty well do whatever brings in money on the side." He studied her face.

July sighed. "That must be why Mr. Bryan told me God smiled on me."

"Well, I believe God smiled on us by bringing you here," said Grams. "Do you want to come inside?"

July gazed up to the tall attic window. There must have been twelve little box panes. Shutters framed both sides. The setting sun glared on the glass, but where one square was missing she thought she glimpsed something move. "You the only ones that live here?" July asked.

"And you," Grams added. "Here, I'll take you in and show you around."

Gramps rubbed his chin, "I'll leave you ladies to it while I go do the chores. It won't take me too long." He tipped his straw hat and headed around to the side of the house.

July followed Grams up on the porch and across the wooden slats. Grams pulled open the screen door and held it with her foot while she turned the knob on the carved door to push it open. "You don't lock the door?" July asked.

"Not in little Plevna, Kansas. Why, everyone knows everyone else. They even know when you're not home and where you've gone. Just about the time I locked it, your gramps would need to get in."

"You could lock it and hide a spare key," suggested July.

"The population of Plevna would probably know how to find the spare key better than I'd remember where I hid it." Grams's laughter sounded like a giggle to July.

"July, this is really the back of the house, but it is where we come in most of the time. Even company usually comes here first." The door opened to a small kitchen that centered about a square mahogany table. On a doily in the middle of the table, an array of welcoming lilacs spilled over the mouth of a quart jar. There was a wood cooking stove and a sink with a pump handle. A few cabinets graced the blue-painted plaster walls. Beneath the staircase on the far wall sat a heavy, wooden icebox. July's eyes traveled up the staircase until it turned the corner. She couldn't help but wonder where she would be sleeping tonight.

Grams interrupted her thoughts. "July, are you okay?"

July nodded.

"We'll look upstairs in a little bit. Let me show you the rest of downstairs." Grams walked through a double doorway. "This is the living room."

Flowered wallpaper had been glued to the plaster walls in here, but it was worn. It looked like Gramps had nailed it in place more than once. There was a bench seat under a bay window that beckoned readers with books. Wooden rockers and latch-hooked rugs were strewn about the rest of the room. From here Grams led July under an arched doorway trimmed with thick molded woodwork.

"And this is the parlor. People who don't know us well come to these doors." Etched glass windows decorated the double front doors. In this room the hardwood floors shone, inviting July to slip and slide across. An upright piano was against the far wall, and there was a stuffed settee under another bright bay window. Two embroidered chairs sat on either side of a tall lamp made from some kind of animal's horns.

Sandra Waggoner

July began to feel she should be tip-toeing about this house. From the outside it didn't look so big, but it was huge.

"And here is where Gramps and I sleep." Grams walked to a pair of massive wooden doors that almost went to the ceiling. She took hold of brass handles on both sides and pushed. July's mouth dropped open as the heavy doors slid inside the walls. A canopy bed stood against airy windows. The lightweight curtains fluttered. A blue patchwork quilt draped the four-poster bed.

July threw her hands over her mouth and sank to the cold hardwood floor. Grams crossed to her side, "Honey, are you alright?"

July shook her head. "No. I have never been in a mansion before. I don't know how to be here."

Grams sat on the floor beside her. "Oh, July, this is not a mansion. There are only four rooms downstairs, and two bedrooms upstairs. This is far from being a mansion. Why, we don't even have an indoor privy. We have a two-hole outhouse. Does that make you feel better?"

July shrugged, "My mama and I never lived in a house before. We just lived in a room in someone else's house when we could afford it."

Grams gasped. "Oh, how I wish we had known. We didn't know where your mama was, and we didn't even know you existed. July, we would have taken you in."

"But would you have taken Mama back?" July whispered. "She was afraid you wouldn't. Sometimes she cried because she missed you so badly. Sometimes I begged her please to come to you. I kept telling her you probably still loved her, but she told me she couldn't go home; she couldn't back up time."

July could see Grams was trying not to cry again. "July, July, July. We would have taken your mama, our May June. We didn't care what she had done; we will always love her, and we miss her so much. Honey, there is a hole in my heart your mama took when she left, and it will always be there." Grams wrapped her arms around the little girl and rocked her.

July snuggled in Grams's arms. Grams seemed much stronger than her mama had ever been. July was always the one holding mama and rocking her. This was different. It was warm and secure, and she liked it.

That was how Gramps found them, two molded into a lump of one. "A chair is much more comfortable," he said.

"Yes, it would be wouldn't it, July. Yet, the floor seems to be where I was needed, Ezra, and I think I'll be here until you can help me to my feet." Grams stretched out her legs and rubbed them.

July smiled as Gramps unwound the two of them and helped his wife to her feet.

"How about supper, May?" he asked.

"Sounds good. We're having leftovers, so I'll get it on the table if you'll show July the upstairs of our *mansion*. You can let her pick out which room she wants."

Gramps chuckled. "Mansion? It's a long ways from being a mansion."

"*Mansion* is what July called it, so *mansion* I guess it will be," Grams laughed.

Gramps and Grams seemed like happy people, July thought. This might not be so bad. She had known it would be better than the orphanage. The streets had been better than the orphanage, except she didn't have to scrounge about for food all the time and dodge the police.

Gramps interrupted her thoughts. "Upstairs it is."

So she would be upstairs by herself. Or would she? She remembered the movement at the attic window.

"Well, let's go, little one," he held his hand out to her.

As they came through the kitchen, Grams asked, "Ezra, I hung the dishpan on the porch. Would you mind grabbing it for me?"

"Sure thing, May. July, you can head on upstairs. I'll be right behind you." He turned towards the door.

July stood at the bottom of the stairs and looked up. Chills crawled up her spine. She took a step, and sure as shooting, the stairs creaked. She reasoned with herself. She had stayed in alleys before. She could do this. This was not the time to let Grams and Gramps know she was afraid. The stairs were dark with the evening shadows. Slowly she took another step. It was going to be fine. She reached the turn of the stairs and froze. Right before her waved a sheeted figure moaning and groaning. July screamed, half fell, and then tumbled to the bottom of the staircase. From there she crawled and tried to scramble to her feet, but with no luck.

Laughter followed her all the way to the kitchen floor. Over her shoulder she watched a wild-haired boy throw back his sheet and jump from the last few steps. "Got ya!" he roared.

Levi

GRAMS stifled a scream, swirled around and threw her wooden spoon across the room. July was glad she was still on the floor as she felt the breeze when that spoon flew over her head. The ghostly, wild-haired boy wasn't so lucky. The wooden spoon whapped him smack in the nose. He yelled and danced savagely around the room with blood splattering the kitchen floor. "She tried to kill me!" he pointed at July. "She tried to kill me!"

July laughed, but when he targeted his eyes on her, she scrambled to her feet and ran for the door. The screen door slammed against the side of the house as she barreled out the door, shoved past Gramps, and sailed across the porch and down the steps. Somewhere in the dry grass the wild-haired boy caught her. He dove for her, and they dropped to the ground, summersaulting together. July was the unlucky one, ending up smashed underneath. She punched and slugged with all her might. When she finally landed a good solid belt into his already bleeding nose, he slumped and fell.

"Yeow!" he squalled, rolling in a ball over the crisp grass.

July sat up and studied the boy. "You are pathetic. Don't you ever touch me again, or you'll get another five-knuckle sandwich.

Your nose will be so out of shape it will never be the same again. It'll be a walrus snout," she threatened.

By now Gramps was standing over the both of them, his blue eyes sparkling with humor. "Levi, if I've told you once, I've told you a thousand times, not everyone will put up with your pranks. Exactly what were you doing anyway?"

Levi sat up and glared at July. "She didn't have to punch me." He wiped his shirt sleeve across his nose leaving a stripe of bloody red.

"Boy, you jumped on top of the girl. Did you think she would act like your sister? It looks like you had better be watching your P's and Q's around this girl." Gramps stated the facts. "Now, you nearly scared your Grams out of her wits." He pointed over his shoulder to where she stood on the porch with her arms crossed. "Did you hear me, son? You nearly scared Grams out of her wits, and she doesn't need that. Plus, you didn't answer my question. Just what were you doing?"

Levi tipped his head to look up at Gramps. "I was taking a peek at her." He pointed to July. "The sheet part was Celie's idea."

"Sheet part?" Gramps asked.

"I'll tell you about the sheet part." July jumped up from the grass and stood over Levi, nudging him with her foot. "He had that blasted sheet thing over his head trying to look like a ghost. Then he hid around the turn of the stairs and made ghost noises to scare me." July kicked a wad of dry grass at him.

Levi crooked his neck back and forth. "It worked, didn't it, scaredy cat? You were so scared you fell backwards and tumbled down the staircase." He belly laughed.

July shoved her face close to his swollen, bloody nose. "Try it again, Buster, and I'll pound your blasted hide so flat to the ground no one will be able to tell which is ground dirt and which is your boy dirt."

Gramps took a hold of her shoulder to ease her away. "Whoa, now—the both of you. You're cousins, and we can't have cousins waylaying each other every chance they get. We had best be seeking a truce."

July's lips formed a grim line, and she looked up and studied Gramps. "You are a preacher, aren't you?" she said flatly.

Levi laughed. "You'd better get used to it, cousin. You're going to be living preaching every single, blasted day of the week, not just Sundays like the rest of us get."

"Levi, 'blasted' is not acceptable language around here," Gramps reminded him.

He flipped his thumb toward July, "She said it. How come she can get by with it, and I can't?"

"She'll learn. You should already know, young man. Now let's work on that truce," Gramps ordered as he turned and walked to the porch. It was clear he expected them to follow.

Levi got up, stuck his tongue out at July, and ran for the porch to get out of her reach.

July shook her fist in the air just as Gramps checked to see if they were following. "Young lady, that is not a sign of peace."

July glared, then slowly lowered her arm to her side.

Levi grabbed his stomach and bellowed with laughter.

"That's enough, Levi." Gramps flipped a cane-backed chair around and sat with his arms resting on the high back. It worked rather like a pulpit. He motioned for the cousins to sit on the porch boards in front of him.

Grams stood at the screen door. "I reckon everything is under control out here. Levi, when Gramps is done with you, come on in, and we'll clean up that nose. I'll try sponging out the shirt, but I'm not a miracle worker." She slipped into the cool house and let the screen door ease closed behind her.

Gramps began his sermon. "First, the two of you need to tell each other you are sorry."

"But I didn't do anything to him. He started it, and I'm not sorry." July scrunched her eyebrows.

"You punched me in the snoze," Levi argued.

"You deserved that, camel snoze."

"Whoa." Gramps held his hand as if it were a stop sign. "I will agree. Levi pretty much got himself into trouble, but enough is enough. I will not have you two fighting in my front yard, my back-yard or anywhere else. What are people going to think?"

"I don't care what people think," July said.

Levi snickered. "Now you're in for a sermon for sure."

Gramps cleared his throat loudly. "*I* care, and as long as you're living with me, you had better start caring, too."

July's eyes opened wide. *As long as she was living with him? Where would she go?* She only paused an instant. "Yes, sir."

"That's better." Gramps began again, "Now, Levi, since you are the man, I want you to apologize first. It's the right thing to do."

"But ..."

July interrupted him, "I've got the guts to do the 'right thing.' I'm sorry I punched you for scaring me in the mansion, chasing me out of the house, and jumping on top of me in the yard."

"What?" Levi gasped.

Gramps chuckled. "Looks like she got the best of you again, Levi. I think July is just what the doctor ordered for you. Now, son, apologize and shake."

"Sorry," Levi said through clenched teeth.

July could tell he wasn't any more sorry than she was.

"Sure," July spit on her hand and stuck it out to shake. She didn't bother to swipe it on her dress this time. Levi deserved spit.

"No way! I ain't shaking that hand. Did you see that, Gramps? She spit in her hand." Levi scrunched his face in disgust.

"July?" Gramps asked.

"It's how you seal a bargain," she told Gramps.

"I don't want it sealed." Levi shoved his hands in his pockets.

Gramps pounded the back of the cane chair as if it were his Sunday pulpit. "I said to shake."

Levi didn't argue anymore. He gritted his teeth, pulled his hand from his pocket and shook. He could feel the cool hunk of spit as July smeared it all over his palm. Levi crunched her hand tight and whispered so only she could hear, "Next time ..."

"There had better not be a next time, Levi," Gramps said without looking at the boy.

July planted a victory smile on her face just for Levi.

"Now, Levi, go find Grams and get your nose taken care of. July, come with me," Gramps said. "I don't think Grams needs your help with this."

July followed. If cousins were this bad, she would be better off without them. Look at what Levi had done. And if it had been Celie's idea for Levi to scare July, what must that girl be like?

6

Sunday Morning

IT wasn't cold, but July cuddled deeply under the homemade quilt. The bed springs twanged with every breath she took. That was a relief, though, because it helped cover all the other noises of the night—and she had heard every one of them. She wasn't used to sleeping alone, much less having the whole second story to herself. Sure, there were only two rooms, but they had those funny under-the-eave closets which she thought were scarier than the alleys where she had slept. And there was Levi. After he had scared her, she seemed to hear noises from every nook and cranny.

She gazed up through the four poster bed to the ceiling and counted the ornate tin squares. Thirty-five squares; there were five down and seven across. The room wasn't big, yet there were two sets of double windows. It was summer, and she had them all open. The breeze felt good. July smiled. This wasn't the biggest of the two bedrooms upstairs, but it had been her mama's. Somehow it brought her mama to life when Grams told July that the bed was the same one her mama had slept in. The quilt was the same, and even the little framed mirror hanging over crates stacked to make a crude vanity was the same. They were Mama's. "Mama, I love your room, and Gramps and Grams, too," July whispered. "I really think you could have come back to them, and everything would have been fine."

"July," Grams called from the bottom of the stairs, pulling her away from her thoughts. "It's time to get up, July. It's Sunday."

July pulled the quilt over her head. She didn't want to go to church. She couldn't see that the church had ever helped Mama. She had been with Mama when she asked the church people for help, and they had flat out told her to go back where she had come from because she was a disgrace to God. That had been in Kansas City. Maybe this little town would be different, but she didn't expect so.

"July?" Grams called a second time. "July, in this house we come the first time Gramps or I holler."

So much for pretending she was asleep. July peeled off the covers. "Coming." She dropped her feet on the cool floor, scuttled across the wooden boards and ran down the stairs.

"Morning, sunshine," Grams smiled.

"Morning," July muttered in passing. "I got to go." She sprung out the door and ran to the outhouse. She fumbled with the leather latch and threw the door wide, pulling it shut after her.

As she sat down in the outhouse, she watched the sunlight filter through the sliver moon at the top of the door. Mama had called it a smiley moon. It was in a sort of sing-song poem which July sang:

Smiley moon, you're up too soon.
The sun's still in the sky.
Across your face the wild geese race,
Against winter's wind they southward fly.

Somewhere up there with those geese maybe Mama was flying. She sighed and dropped her eyes to the empty seat beside her, only it wasn't empty. Coiled about the hole lay a snake. She didn't know what kind. It didn't matter what kind. It was a snake, and her heart was pounding in her ears. She was done. She jumped away and plastered herself against the outhouse wall.

That was when she heard the snicker from outside. It was a Levi snicker. Her fear whirled into anger. How dare he pull that stunt. There was no way she was going to let him get by with it! The snake must not be poisonous if Levi put it there, and if Levi could handle that snake, so could she. She drew in a deep breath, reached over and snatched up the snake right behind its beady little eyes and pinched hard, that way the snake couldn't swing around and bite her. She cringed as she felt the cold, scaly snake hide, but she held tight. Then she twisted her hand behind her back, slapped the outhouse door wide and marched around the corner to where Levi crouched toward the ground in laughter.

"Levi!" she yelled. With her empty hand she grabbed the nape of his shirt, pulled it wide and dropped the swirling snake down his front. Levi gasped as his eyes popped open. "Help!!" he shouted as he danced across the dusty grass like a Maasai warrior. Without unbuttoning his shirt, Levi yanked it over his head. The squirming snake dropped to the ground and slithered away.

July fell to the ground in laughter. Levi tripped and crashed on top of her, and the rolling war began. Levi smacked, and July pounded. Shouts, yells, grunts and groans burst through the Sunday morning air.

"Stop it! Both of you, stop it!" Grams ordered.

The battle was on, and neither was listening. Levi's nose was busted and bleeding again. July was on the bottom and ready to pound his chin when a blast of cold water cascaded over the both of them. Levi gasped. July gulped.

With fire in her eyes, Grams stood above them, holding an empty bucket. Slowly Levi crawled off of July, and July sat up. They were drenched and muddy, and neither said a word. July was almost afraid to breathe. Grams's face was a storm brewing. "I don't know what happened this time, but I have had enough. This is Sunday morning, God's day, and both of you are a mess. Levi, your mother will have something to say about this, I'm sure. July, we will talk later. Gramps does not like us to be late for church, and it looks like that is exactly what we are going to be—late." Grams turned and marched to the house without looking back.

The porch door slammed, and silence settled. July glared at Levi while he stared after Grams. "She never slams a door," he said. "We're in big trouble."

July's tummy churned. What if Grams changed her mind about keeping July?

"My mama is going to kill me, and it's all your fault, *cousin*. This is my Sunday shirt," Levi yelled.

July stared at Levi. "It's *your* fault, *cousin*. You brought the snake."

Levi spat. "It was only a garter snake. They're not poison. Besides, they don't even have teeth, so they couldn't bite you if they wanted to."

"Well, how would I know that? I came from the city. Most sidewalks and alleys don't have snakes." July jumped up. "Don't ever try that again." She turned and left Levi standing, his wet hair molded to his head and his soggy shirt in his hands.

He shouted after her, "This isn't the end. I don't forget. I get even."

July didn't reply. She trudged up the steps, across the porch, and into the kitchen. The lilacs drooped on the table, and she thought they looked like she felt. "Now I have to take another bath," she told Grams.

Grams shook her head. "No, July, I'm sorry, but there is no time for another bath. We can't heat up that much water that fast. You'll just have to sponge off."

July didn't say a word, but her face said it all. She didn't want to go to church. "I could stay here today. No one will miss me because no one knows I'm alive."

"No, ma'am. This is Plevna, Kansas. We're a little town, and by now everyone inside and outside of Plevna knows you're here. Besides, your gramps would miss you."

July groaned.

"I mean it, young lady. You don't have a choice. We're going to go to church." Grams handed her a washcloth to start 'sponging.'

Still July hesitated.

Grams spread her hands. "You might as well get started, and you can wash up right here in the kitchen. Gramps has already gone to the church. He likes going early on Sundays. He says it gives him time to be alone with God."

In a huff, July peeled off the nightshirt that had come from a stack of Gramps's worn out work shirts. She took the washcloth from Grams. When the job was done, Grams pushed her toward the stairs. "Put on the dress I made, and run a comb through your hair."

"Sundays are not going to be my favorite days." July spat each word, one word per step, as she stomped up the stairs.

"No stomping in this house, young lady," Grams said.

July quit stomping, and she turned to see if Grams were watching. She wasn't there. How did Grams seem to know her very thoughts? She ran across the room, took the comb and yanked it through her tangled hair. After she pulled the flour sack dress in place, July paused in front of the smoky mirror. The little blue flowers sprinkled over the dress made bright the blue of her eyes. She smiled. She had Gramps's eyes, the kind of blue that was like cool water you could wade deep into. Mama's eyes had been more of a faded blue color, maybe even gray-blue, the same as Grams's eyes. July's lashes were thick and dark as was her hair. She shrugged. She could have been pretty if it weren't for the freckles that splattered all over her face. It looked like she had been standing beside a muddy road when an auto sped by. "Oh well," July scrunched up her nose and turned from the mirror. "Mama always promised me the stupid freckles would go away when I got older. I can't wait for older." She took the stairs two at a time.

Grams's arms were crossed. Her pocketbook swung from one elbow, and she clutched her Bible in her arms as she waited at the door. Since it was clear Grams was ready to go, July grabbed a cold biscuit to eat on the way.

They closed the door behind them and headed for the sidewalk. "You had best eat that biscuit fast because it won't pass through the church-house doors," Grams warned.

July replied by shoving the rest of the biscuit into her mouth and wiping the crumbs from her lips, chin and the front of her dress.

Grams shook her head in dismay.

Several yards down the long block, July noticed an unpainted house that looked to have been grand at one time. It had two tall, rounded, rock towers as a castle would have. A stone porch stretched from one tower to the other, and stone walkways circled the house, forming pathways across the dry dirt. The windows were bare, looking hollow and eerie. All the shrubs about the place had died, and dust had settled over everything. "Wow, who lives there?"

Grams stopped. "No one that I know of. It's been for sale for ten or eleven years, but something has happened to the 'for sale' sign." There was a heap of dry sod where the sign must have been. Grams seemed to be staring far into the distance.

"Is that it up on the porch?" July asked.

"What?" Grams brought her attention back to the little girl.

"The sign. Is that it up on the porch?" July asked again.

The wooden sign was still chained and swung lopsided to the post that had held it in the ground. It was wedged where the bay window protruded from the wall, but it was backwards so no one could read it.

"I expect it could be. Hmm, I didn't think anyone would ever buy that house." Grams seemed puzzled and spoke more to herself than to July.

"Why? It needs paint on the wooden part, but most of the house is made out of rock. It would be crazy to paint rocks. That is some castle-house," July whistled.

"Let's just say the 'castle-house' has quite a shady history." Grams continued staring at the house.

"Shady history? Did somebody get killed there?" July asked.

Grams turned to July. "Let's get to church. We're already late."

July was on a mission. "I'm right, aren't I. Somebody got killed there, didn't they? Grams, you've got to tell me."

"July, I don't have to tell you a thing, and it would probably be better if you didn't know."

"Just tell me if someone was killed, please?" July begged. "I promise I'll never say another word about not going to church, ever."

"Not exactly killed," Grams held up her hand. "But there will be no more talk until after church. Now, let's speed it up."

July couldn't wait until after church for more reasons than one.

They could hear the singing even before they turned the corner where the church stood. It wasn't a very big church, but Plevna wasn't a very big town. There was a steeple piercing high in the sky with one huge bell hanging in the tower. As they went up the steps, July swiped her hands down the sides of her dress to get rid of the clammy feeling. She could see that about all the pews were full. She wondered if they had all come to see what she looked like. At least Grams had gotten the flour sack dress made so she didn't have to wear her orphanage outfit, and her hair was combed. July twisted her mouth, expecting the worst. Nobody had better say anything about the freckles.

"There will be peace in the valley for me, some day," the congregation sang. July could only hope she would have peace. Peace in the valley would be fine, but peace here would be better, and she wished it would be today.

The singing was over, the people had sat down, and Gramps was speaking. Grams pushed her up the church steps. July took a deep breath and paused at the door.

"Go on," Grams whispered.

Timidly, July took a step inside and was glad for the shadows after the sunshine outside. She didn't even look around to see if she knew anyone because that would only be Mr. Bryan and Levi. She didn't particularly want to see Levi again. She reached for the ring about her neck and patted it.

"July, we're in luck. I think there is a place on the back pew. You slide in, and I'll follow," Grams said.

July didn't look to one side or the other. She just sat down and slid. Grams scooted in after her and nudged her to go a little further. When July did, she bumped into the lady next to her. "Oops, sorry," July whispered.

The orange flower bobbed on the hat as the lady turned. Her eyebrows rose almost to her hairline. "So it's you?" she hissed. July could smell stale coffee on the woman's breath.

July felt her heart pounding in her ears. It was The Dragon.

The Dragon wasn't finished with July. She stretched her hand over and clutched July's knee. With clipped words she said, "I want to talk to you after the service, young lady."

July stared straight ahead and tried to ignore the woman. Gramps was preaching, but she had no idea what he was saying. From across the aisle, a wet wad of paper thunked her in the forehead. She whipped her head around. There sat Levi snickering. July ducked as another wad flew her way. She smirked when it missed, but sucked in a panicked breath when it smacked Mrs. Drunyon on the cheek.

"Of all the nerve!" The Dragon leaned level with the terrified girl and growled. Her claws dug into July's arm as she stood and yanked the little girl to her feet. "How dare you," she mouthed. "You are coming with me this instant." She pushed July over Grams and into the aisle.

By now everyone had stopped listening to Gramps, and worse yet, they all turned to watch the back-row drama. Levi was laughing almost out loud. As the shock wore off Grams, she jumped to her feet and grabbed The Dragon's purse handle, yanking her away from July.

Gramps's loudest preaching voice bellowed over the congregation. "May, what is going on back there?"

"I don't know, Ezra." Grams tossed one hand up in the air like a bucking bronc rider while being towed after the woman hanging on to her granddaughter.

The Dragon was dragging July toward the door. July was struggling to free her arm. "Let me go," she insisted.

"Give me the ring," The Dragon ordered. She whipped the girl around and pressed herself face to face with July.

Levi came to the rescue from behind. He plunged into the woman, knocking her away from July. "That is my cousin, and no one but me treats her that way."

Some peace in the valley. July tensed as she pressed her hands to her hot cheeks.

Celie

Grams grabbed the porch pillar, but Mrs. Drunyon stumbled down the steps, caught her heel and sprawled on the church yard. Her hat was hanging over one eye, and her hair splayed around her face. The hem of her dress hiked just above one rolled knee-high stocking, making her legs look rather like skinny chicken legs with heavy shoes hanging on the ends. Her arms propped her in a sitting position with her purse swinging from one shoulder. The eye left uncovered by the hat sparked as she glared at Levi and July. Her nostrils flared. "Cousins?" she fumed. "That doesn't surprise me in the least. Whoever is responsible for the two of you needs to have a lesson in discipline. You are a disgrace to all of mankind."

Levi's eyes were huge. "July, you know that woman?"

July smiled. "Levi, meet Mrs. Drunyon. She taught at the orphanage, and she was my chaperone, the one who brought me here on the train."

Levi stepped closer to Grams and further away from the woman on the ground.

How and when the congregation had poured from the church July didn't know, but they were now gathered on the lawn around the scene. Gramps pushed to the front of the steps, and July was glad to be hidden behind him.

"Well," Gramps began, "we've not had a Sunday quite like this before, Honey." He squeezed Grams's shoulder as he brushed past her. "But I can follow my people anywhere to finish a sermon, even out on the front lawn," Gramps chuckled. "Someone help Mrs. Drunyon to her feet. Are you hurt, Ma'am?"

A couple of men stooped to raise Mrs. Drunyon gently to her feet.

Gramps walked down the steps to stand in front of the lady. "Ma'am, are you hurt?" he asked again.

"So, you are still the pastor of this church?" she asked as she brushed dry grass from her dress.

"Yes, Ma'am, Mrs. Drunyon. Pastor Calendar at your service." He held out his hand to shake with the woman.

"Ezra Calendar?" She yanked her head from him to July to Levi and back again. "You are the grandpa to that girl, aren't you?" She paused. "The apple doesn't fall far from the tree, does it?" The Dragon swept a deeper look over Gramps. "I didn't recognize you in a tie. If you'd had on those overalls from the train station, I would have known you right off, Ezra. You're the grandpa to the hellion, aren't you?"

"She is my granddaughter, Helen, and one of the apples of my eye." He looked at her more carefully. "Thank you for chaperoning July from the orphanage. I see you're wearing the same hat."

Tension was building, and the people tightened their circle around the two. It began to feel like a face-off.

Mrs. Drunyon was a tall woman only inches shorter than Gramps. She leaned in closer to him and poked her finger in the middle of his chest. "Pastor Calendar, I am glad to find you are still a man of God. That granddaughter of yours has something of mine. If you will make her return it, I'll not charge her with theft."

It seemed the whole town of Plevna, Kansas held their breath, waiting for Gramps's answer. He stood to his full height. "Mrs. Drunyon, July has explained to her grandmother and me that this 'something' is a ring—her mother's wedding ring. It is the only thing her mother could leave her in passing. I don't really believe you or anyone else would begrudge her that dear of a possession."

Mrs. Drunyon narrowed her eyes and poked Gramps again. "Right is right. It doesn't belong to her, and I want it back."

Carefully Gramps brushed her hand away. "Ma'am, I will not force my granddaughter to give away what is rightfully hers. What is *right* is *right!*"

Then he turned his back on Mrs. Drunyon and walked to stand on the church porch to address the audience. "Ladies and gentlemen, church is over for this Sunday. Please be much in prayer for the situations of the day. God bless you, and I thank you all."

Warmth rushed through July. At that moment she loved her Gramps.

The Dragon didn't. She had to have the last word. "Tomorrow, Monday morning, I will be pressing charges, and that little wayward child will be going to reform school. You won't be able to hide her, and she can't run away. They will have her under lock and key. Don't say I didn't warn you." With those words, she turned and marched over the dry ground, billowing dust clouds with each step. July called them smoke clouds because that fit The Dragon better.

The crowd stepped back for the woman, and no one spoke until she was out of hearing range.

"Who was that?" someone asked.

"No one has ever talked to Pastor Calendar that way before," a woman added.

A man shook his head and whistled with disbelief.

"I think I've seen her before," another said.

"I hope I never see her again," a girl vowed.

July couldn't agree more and looked to see who it was. The girl was about July's age. Her strawberry hair curled in every direction, and her green eyes laughed with her smile. Freckles colored her face like mountains marked the map of Colorado. July knew who she was—this had to be Levi's twin sister—the girl version of Levi.

While all of the adults were discussing the strange turn of events, the girl marched over to July and stuck her hand out. "I'm your cousin, Celie. I've heard you have been giving Levi a run for his money, not that he really has any money. I'm glad to meet you."

July studied her while they shook. Levi had said the ghost thing was Celie's idea, so July didn't know whether to trust her or not.

Celie babbled on. "I couldn't wait to meet you, but Mama said to give you a few days to settle in before we bombard you. Are you settled yet? Mama says it will probably take you a while since you came from an orphanage, and you probably aren't used to normal people. Plus, right now, Mama is not sure you are really you."

"Wait," July interrupted. "What do you mean, 'I'm not used to people'? I've been around people all my life. I've even slept with people at the orphanage. And what do you mean by 'you are really you'? Who else would I be?"

"Well," Celie smiled, "that is Mama for you. She never even really knew your mother, June. Well, maybe she knew her a little, but not very well. However, she was sure June didn't ever have a baby."

July put her hands on her hips. "And who am I supposed to be if I am not June's girl?"

Celie laughed. "That's exactly what I asked Mama."

"What did your mama say?"

Again Celie laughed. "July, I love my mother, but she is a tad bit uppity."

July thought her cousin could beat around the bush better than anyone she had ever met. "Celie, what did your mama say?"

Celie pressed her lips together. "I didn't want to tell you this, but she thinks maybe you are street trash—*alley trash*."

July's mouth dropped open. Never had she been called alley trash to her face before. Her fists tightened, and she drew in a deep breath.

Celie held up her hand. "Wait. I don't think that, July. I'm glad you're here, and I think we are going to be more than cousins. I think we are going to be best friends."

July was pretty good at knowing people, but Celie was different. Maybe she was more honest than most people she met. Maybe she was fibbing.

"July," Celie continued, "let's hug. And let's promise to always be honest and friends. After all, I told you what Mama said. That is honesty for sure. I think that deserves some consideration on your part."

July wasn't used to a bunch of hugging, and she sure wasn't used to Celie. Yet, it would be great if she were truly a friend. She paused before she let Celie give her a hug.

Celie laughed. "July, it wouldn't hurt you to hug back, you know."

When Celie let go, July looked her in the eye. "What about the sheet?" July wanted to catch any clue she might find as to whether Celie had been the mastermind behind draping Levi in that ghostly manner the day she arrived.

"Is this a trick question?" Celie asked.

July studied her face, but she couldn't find the tiniest hint that Celie knew anything about it. There was no blink or anything to give her away. July decided to give her the benefit of the doubt for now, but she would still be very careful.

Levi came running from behind. "July," he grabbed her arm. "I followed her."

July whipped around. "The Dragon? You followed The Dragon?"

Celie furrowed her auburn brows. "Who?"

Levi ignored his sister and nodded. "You've got to come and see."

"See who, Levi?" Celie asked again.

July answered. "The Dragon."

Celie raised her shoulders. "Who is The Dragon?"

"The Dragon, Celie. She's the woman who dragged July out of the church. That's The Dragon." He turned back to July. "You've got to come. Hurry!"

"Wait a minute. I have to ask Gramps and Grams if I can go with you. I can't run off and leave without telling them."

"I'm coming, too," Celie added. "Here, let me tell Grams."

"Grams, can Levi and I walk July home?" Celie's smile revealed a delightful dimple.

Grams smiled. "That would be nice, Celie, and I'll bet July would like that. Gramps and I will be home in a while."

Levi was antsy. "You won't believe this. Come on."

Celie giggled. "Let's go."

July decided maybe Celie was going to be okay.

Levi dipped down an alley, through a dead brush-covered backyard, around a corner, over a fence and down the street. The girls raced to keep him in sight. When July and Celie caught up with him, he was bent over holding onto his legs above his knees and trying to catch his breath.

"Are you alright, Levi?" July asked.

He nodded as he stood. His chest was heaving. "There," he pointed.

July gasped. It was the empty castle house she had asked Grams about this morning.

Celie held her hands over her mouth. "Oh, oh, oh!" was all she could say.

Levi's hair flew in all directions as he bobbed his head up and down. "That house. That is the house where The Dragon went."

"Grams said it was for sale. Do you think she bought it?" July's gut felt heavy. "Do you think The Dragon is going to live right here in Plevna, Kansas—the same town I live in?"

"Could be," Levi mumbled.

Celie was still 'oh, oh, oh-ing,' and her eyes were wild.

Levi looked at her and nodded. "Celie gets it."

"What? What does Celie get?" July asked.

Levi pointed. "That place. That place is haunted. A man killed himself there. It was in the garage right over the family Model-T Ford."

July's heart was racing. She slapped her hand to her forehead. "Was he a banker?"

"Yeah, he was a banker. How did you know?" Levi asked.

July closed her eyes in dread. "And he hung himself?"

"Yes," Levi whispered.

"And he left a note under the windshield wiper?" July asked him.

"Hey, did Grams and Gramps tell you those things?" Levi asked.

Celie started dancing. "Oh, oh, oh ..." Celie pointed toward the front door and started dancing.

The door thundered open, and The Dragon tromped across the stone porch.

"Run! Run! Run!" Celie yelled. Yet she stood in place and danced in the grass.

Levi didn't need to be told twice. He was gone.

July sped away but turned in time to see The Dragon stomping toward Celie and gaining speed as she got closer.

July whipped about, latched onto Celie's arm, and tugged. "Celie, you've got to run!" she yelled.

The Dragon swiped at July's dress and barely missed.

Like a bolt of lightning, Celie panicked, jumped loose from her spot and ran, dragging July away from the clutches of The Dragon.

8

Something Inside

JULY was tucked under the quilt even though she didn't need it. The nights cooled, but not really enough for a quilt. She couldn't get used to being upstairs all alone. The house moaned and creaked at night. Out the window she could see stars twinkling through the branches of Grams's catalpa tree. She smiled as she imagined the tree as black lace over velvet smattered with rhinestone stars. July couldn't wait to describe this to Grams because she was pretty proud of that tree. Grams had brought it from her home place, and that was all the way from Rocky Branch, Louisiana. Grams gave that little tree water every day. July guessed she had been doing that for a long time because the tree was taller than this two-story house.

July sighed. She felt the call of the outhouse, and she knew if she didn't answer it now, she would be forced to later in the night. She threw the quilt to the side and crawled out of bed. She tip-toed down the creaky stairs so she wouldn't wake anyone. When she came to the turn in the staircase, she stopped. Grams and Gramps were not asleep. They must be at the kitchen table talking. July heard the name of her lawyer friend, Sam Bryan, and listened.

"Ezra, what did Sam Bryan say?" Grams asked.

"He told me the old woman got herself a lawyer," Gramps spoke low.

"Ezra, you can't call her an old woman. I know she is not a very nice lady, but you still can't call her an old woman. What if the grandkids heard you?" Grams scolded him lightly.

Gramps chuckled. "The grandkids aren't going to hear me call her an old woman. Besides, May, I call it like I see it. I s'pose there are worse things I could call her than an old woman."

"Ezra, you had better not. You are the pastor," Grams reminded him.

"And that old woman ought to be glad I am. There are things I could have said today. It's a good thing I let the Lord have control."

"Now, young man ..." Grams began.

"May, I haven't been called a young man for a long time." He laughed, and Grams joined him.

When the laughter floated away, Grams continued: "Seriously, I'm worried. What did Sam say?"

"The old ... excuse me, I mean *Mrs. Drunyon* was not able to get the orphanage lawyer to take her case because the orphanage gave Mrs. Drunyon her walking papers."

May interrupted, "She got fired?"

"Seems so," Gramps said.

"Why?"

Gramps sighed. "It's a long story, but the gist of it goes something like this: When Sam told the orphanage lawyer Mrs. Drunyon had threatened July with a passenger's cane—in front of a crowd of witnesses no less—the lawyer refused to take the case. He also advised the orphanage to avoid further complications by relieving Mrs. Drunyon of her teaching duties. I guess they took their lawyer's advice."

"Ezra, does that mean she has moved here?" Grams was concerned.

"May, you know who she is," said Gramps.

July could feel the heaviness as Grams spoke. "But it has been almost twelve years, Ezra. I thought it could be forgotten."

"May. May, honey, *we* haven't forgotten. I doubt anyone else has forgotten either," Gramps said.

"That old woman." Grams talked softly, but July could still hear the words.

Gramps laughed. "May, if I can't call her an old woman, you can't do it either."

Grams giggled. "I know. I'm sorry, Ezra."

July peeked around the corner of the stairs as Gramps slid his chair closer to Grams. "Don't tell me you're sorry. You'll have to tell the Lord."

July watched Grams smile. It took years from her face. It made her look even more like Mama. July felt a sick hole in her heart.

Grams looked to the ceiling. "I'm sorry, Lord." Then her eyes twinkled as she turned them to Gramps. "Is that better?"

Gramps chuckled.

"Ezra," Grams said, "I'm worried. Can Mrs. Drunyon win? Oh, I'm not worried about the ring. Knowing our June, the ring is most likely worthless. But can the State send July to a reform school? What if July runs away?"

"Don't forget, May, we have a big God."

"But I can't lose July. I can't lose her. I lost her mother, and that about killed me. I think I would die if I lost July. She's a part of us, Ezra; I love her. I *can't* lose her." Grams was crying.

July wasn't far from tears. She had to be careful, or she would sniffle, and then they would know she had been listening. All of a sudden, she didn't care if they knew. She plunged down the rest of the stairs and stood across the table from them. "You don't have to worry. I'm not going to run away. I don't have anywhere to go, and this is the best place I've ever been."

Grams and Gramps were stunned. A time of silence passed before Gramps asked, "How long have you been listening, young lady?"

July knew she could be in trouble, but she didn't care. "For a while. I've been listening for a while. I heard some good things, and I heard some bad things. I heard you say God is good, and I heard you say The Dragon lost her job and that she lives here in Plevna now."

"July, I assume you are referring to Mrs. Drunyon?" Gramps did not smile. "I don't think calling her *The Dragon* is going to work around this house. Am I understood?"

July blew upwards, making her hair split from her forehead. "You called her an old woman."

Gramps never let his eyes leave her face. "Yes, Ma'am, I did, and I think we both know I was wrong. I will not call her that again, and you will not call her The Dragon again."

It was an order, and July knew she had no choice but to agree. She replied with a nod. "Mrs. Drunyon. It will be Mrs. Drunyon, but there is something, some secret you know about her. That much I can tell. What is it?"

Gramps patted the chair next to him. "July come and sit a spell."

July hesitated. Was it better to be sitting down when a secret was revealed? It was if it were bad news. That's what people always said when they had bad news: *"Have a seat."* That's what the policeman said when her mama died. That's what the case worker had told her when she was going to be put into an orphanage. So bad news must be coming. She pulled the chair from beneath the table and sat across from both of them. She wanted to see them face to face. You can tell a lot by watching people's faces. "Now you can let me know the bad news."

Gramps was the one doing the talking. "First, we have a few questions."

"About the ring and Mrs. Drunyon?" July asked.

"Maybe later, but right now we would like to know about our daughter, May June. We have heard very little since the day she left us."

July traced the pattern in the wood on the mahogany table. Finally, she rested her chin in her hands. "Mama wasn't very strong. She was always getting sick. Mostly we lived in a room somewhere and snuck out at night when we couldn't make the room rent. Then Mama would catch odd jobs and earn enough to get another room. We would keep that room as long as the job lasted. We lived that way over and over again. She always promised things would be better when Daddy came back. I think I was about three the last time I saw Daddy. After a few years, I didn't think Daddy would ever come back, but it seemed to help Mama if I pretended to believe her."

Grams whispered. "Honey, do you know who your daddy is?"

"I never heard his name. It was always just *Daddy*," said July.

"Do you remember what he looked like?" Gramps asked.

July let her hands slide up her cheeks. "He was big. His hands were huge when he held mine. But I don't remember much else."

"Tell us what you do know, July. It will help all three of us," Gramps said gently.

"We mostly lived in rooms until Mama got sick. Then she couldn't clean or iron or cook for anyone anymore, so we lost whatever room we were in. The only place left to stay was in alleys—or better yet, empty buildings if we could find them. Usually we would pick an alley behind some cafe or grocery story. It made it easier to find food."

Silent tears were streaming down Grams's face, and she kept wringing her hands. July could tell Gramps had inside tears. Those were the worst kind because they try to work themselves out, and it rips you apart trying to keep them inside. Then when they do get out, there is always flood damage. Those tears have their own plan. They don't pay attention to yours.

July is Coming

July looked into the past. "The winters were the worst. It was hard to stay warm. I think that is what finally wore Mama down. That and the police. The police wanted to take me away and put me in an orphanage, but I couldn't let that happen. I had to take care of Mama. The police weren't going to take care of Mama, and they plain told me the orphanage wouldn't take Mama in with me. After that we had to keep moving to stay hidden from the police."

Grams's voice was shaky. "Oh, July, why didn't you let us know? We would have taken you both."

July threw her hands into the air. "I didn't even know you, and what if you had been like the police? What if you just wanted us to disappear and pretend we never were? I would have been better off to never know you than to know you didn't want me. Besides, I didn't know where you were, and there was no way Mama was going to tell me. She wouldn't even whisper that secret to me before she died."

"Oh, July ..." Grams choked on the words and couldn't finish.

Gramps shook his head in despair as he gently put his arm around Grams before he spoke to his granddaughter. "You thought no one wanted you?"

"I knew Mama wanted me, and she was forever telling me God wanted me, but God is pretty hard to see. And Mama is gone. That doesn't leave much." July seemed far away and helpless.

In a small voice Gramps spoke. "July, God does want you. He loves you, and I think he brought you to us so we could introduce you to him."

July returned from memories that had taken her far away, and she studied Gramps's face. His sky blue eyes held water waves of tears that could flood at any time. He was the nicest man she had ever met. "I believe God is here. I can't see him, but I feel him when I am close to you and Grams."

"That is because God is inside of Grams and me—in our hearts, July." Gramps let that soak in before he continued. "July ..."

She interrupted, "What? Wait. You said God is *inside* of you?"

"Yes," Gramps answered.

"How did God get inside of you?" July asked in disbelief.

"It's easy, July. I know you believe in God. Lots of people believe in God, but they don't have him inside of them."

July could see that. With most people she knew, it didn't feel much like being around God, much less like having him in their heart.

"July, God will not be an uninvited guest. He won't be a part of you if you haven't asked him to be," Gramps said.

July toyed with her bottom lip while she thought about what Gramps had said. "Gramps, I'm only ten, but I've kind of noticed that God really only likes good people." She struggled for a moment before she went on. "I'm not a good person. I've snuck out on room rent. I've kicked policemen, and I've stolen food and other things. I stole a blanket from a store last year to keep us warm, and I still would rather call Mrs. Drunyon 'The Dragon.' " Tears flooded down July's cheeks. "It's too late for me. I'm a bad person. God doesn't want me."

"Oh, yes he does, June July Calendar." July didn't know when he had left his seat, but Gramps was kneeling on the floor beside her. "God only loves sinners—the bad people—because we all are those people. The only one on the face of the earth without sin was Jesus Christ, God in flesh. He died for sinners, *the bad people*. That is you and me, July. We are the bad people."

July looked at her grandpa, her eyes wide. "God loves the bad people?"

"It doesn't make sense, does it? But then God doesn't think with our little, tiny minds. God feels with his heart. You see, he calls us children when we belong to him. As a parent there is nothing your children can do to separate them from your love. July, what could you have done that would have made your mama quit loving you?"

Like the first ray of morning light, July understood. "Nothing. Mama would have loved me no matter what."

"Exactly. No matter what. And God is even more loving than your mama." Gramps's eyes shone. "What about it, July? Would you like to invite God to be a part of you?"

July wiped her cheeks, never letting her eyes leave his. Finally, she nodded.

"Go on. Just ask him," Gramps encouraged.

July leaned in close to look into Gramps's blue eyes before she bowed her head to pray. "God, I know you are in there, inside of Gramps somewhere. I don't know how, but I can feel you there every time I am around Gramps. What I am asking is if you would be inside of me the same way you're in Grams and Gramps. I want to tell you, I'm sorry for the bad things ... and honest ... I will try to clean up and be really good, so it won't be such an awful place for you to stay like an alley or something. Well, I don't guess I can give you a spit-shake to seal my promise, so I'm thinking that's it, God." In a tiny, sweet voice she whispered, "Thank you," as if it were the last cookie crumb.

Gramps took her in his arms and gave her something that must have equaled the very best daddy hug she could remember. It was the best place in the world she had ever been.

The Butter Bet

"**B**UT ... I ... I don't really want to," Celie looked at the old, dark shed that stood in front of them.

"Celie, it will be fine," Levi said.

Celie shook her head. "I don't think it is fine to trespass on someone's property, Levi."

"It isn't trespassing if she doesn't own the property," Levi reasoned.

"But she's there," his sister said.

Levi shrugged. "Okay, Celie. I guess you could stand out here and be our lookout for The Dragon."

"What? Lookout? For The ... The ... The Dragon?" she stuttered.

"Sure, you could just whistle to let us know if The Dragon is coming," Levi said.

Celie shook her head. "There is no way that is going to happen. I'm not going to be a sitting duck for that woman."

"Good. That means you're coming with us. Right, July?" Levi asked.

July pulled her eyes away from the old shed and looked at the two of them. She hadn't even been listening to her cousins' bickering.

The shed hadn't seen paint in years, and the building seemed to be an afterthought to the amazing castle house. The wooden shutters were boarded up, and the door had a chain with a padlock. Dead brush stood like wiry whiskers around the sides of the building. An old bucket, half full of rusty bolts, rested beside the door. On the alley side, the branches of an ancient cedar tree rubbed the side of the shed.

"Come on, let's get this over with," July said. This was a bet she had lost to Levi, and betting was something else she was sure she shouldn't do, but Levi would tell Grams and Gramps about it if she didn't keep her side of the bargain. Somehow she was sure Levi had cheated, but how? She couldn't figure that out. He ate a whole block of butter. He didn't even take a drink of water. July felt like gagging as she remembered him sliding great huge gulps from a spoon and swallowing them whole. He hadn't even winced.

July made the decision. "The door is chained, so I guess we'll have to try a window."

"But the windows are nailed shut," Celie protested.

"Not all of them," Levi pointed. "Look up there, behind the tree."

"Sure enough," July whistled. All old sheds had them. It wasn't really a two-story building, but there was always rafter space for storing old things and junk. "It will be easy. We'll shinny up the tree and climb in the window."

Levi chuckled. "You first. You lost the bet."

July glared at him.

It was Celie who held back. "I don't like cedar trees. They're prickly everywhere, and they get you all sticky with cedar sap."

"Then don't come, Celie," he teased snidely. "Remember, you can always be the look-out."

"All right, I'm coming. But next time he does the butter bet, July, talk to me first. Levi loves butter."

July glared at him. "You love butter?"

Levi laughed. "It's almost as good as ice cream."

"You cheater." July planted her hands on her hips.

Levi shrugged, "A bet is a bet, loser."

July felt fire burning inside, but she would get even. Levi was right as far as a bet being a bet. She would stand by her word. Later, Levi would pay, though. She turned back to the shed.

Like the rest of the place, the cedar had not been cared for. The lower limbs brushed the ground, and July had to wiggle her way into the tree. No matter how she turned, she was slapped by branches, but the cedar did have a nice smell. "Okay, guys, follow me," she called.

Celie was next because there was no way she wanted to be last. That left Levi to be the caboose. July was glad to finally reach the window. That tree was a jungle all by itself. She had to let her eyes adjust to the dark inside the shed. A few rays of light filtered through the splits in the roof, and dust particles flicked in the streaming sunlight. Dust lay over everything like silt. For years this place had been sealed closed. July felt eerie fingers trickle over her body. That must be what it would feel like stepping into one of those mausoleums she had seen at the cemetery where Mama was buried. The very air she breathed was heavy as death.

No one spoke. Finally, Celie whispered, "This is too creepy for me. Let's go."

"No, we came here to find some answers, and we're not going until we get them," Levi said. But July noticed a tremor in his voice.

"Then let's do it." July crawled across the rafters, and both Celie and Levi followed.

"Look," Celie pointed below them.

Like thick skin, dust covered a Model-T automobile.

Levi whistled and turned to Celie. "Right there," Levi gently touched the place where Celie rested her foot. "Right there would have been where he tied the rope."

"To hang himself? Oh! Oh! Oh!" Celie scrambled from the spot and sat with her knees up to her chin and her hands slapped over her mouth. "Oh, oh, oh," she continued.

"Levi, quit it," July warned. "As far as I'm concerned, this takes care of the butter bet I lost. You wanted to see if the Model-T was still here. We all see the Model-T. All you wanted us to do was see if it. Right? Well, here it is. See?"

Levi laughed. "Then you two can wait here because I want to check things out a little closer. Clues, that's what I'm looking for." Levi inched toward the ladder.

"The clues are going to be all gone. Police have taken anything that would be evidence in the case. And what if you get caught?" July asked.

"What if *we* get caught, you mean. I'm not here alone. Besides, the place is locked up. We had to crawl through that window, and no one I know is going to do that. Nobody's been here in years." Levi chuckled at how smart he was.

July thought if she weren't with him, she would hope he got caught. Celie had quit her "oh's" but was still rocking back and forth. Levi dropped to the dirt floor and crossed to the auto. He stretched out his hand apprehensively and clutched the door handle. July heard him whisper, "One, two, three …" Levi yanked the door open, sounding as if it were a loud clap of thunder. He scooted into the driver's seat and slammed the door shut. A cloud of dust billowed. He tinkered with the windshield wiper and mirror on the outside of the door before he clutched the steering wheel and drove into his own dream world.

July was too curious. The need to be at his side was overwhelming. She scuttled to the ladder, but before she hit the top rung, the building heaved. July froze while her heart pounded in her chest. The door shook again and again with violent blows. Celie began crying silently. Levi was having so much fun he didn't notice. July thought he must be speeding over a mighty bumpy road in his imagination because it felt like the very building was bucking down the worst road ever.

July struggled to breathe. Somehow she had to get to Levi and get him out of that auto. Before she could move, the door slammed open and whapped the side of the shed. Daylight streamed through the doorway, shadowing the image of a tall wiry-haired woman with an axe raised in her hands, ready to strike.

"Levi!" July yelled.

Levi, his eyes wide, yanked his head around toward the light that shone through the door. The shadowy image in the door screamed and threw the axe so hard it shook the wall as it stuck into the wood. "Maxworth!" She grabbed her heart, groaned, and sank to the sod. It was The Dragon, and she wasn't moving.

July scrambled down the ladder and over to the crumpled body. Levi looked as if he had seen a ghost. He fumbled with the handle, trying to get out of the automobile. When it finally opened, he raced to July's side. "Is she dead?"

Celie was still rocking back and forth up in the rafters.

"Dear Lord, I hope not," July reverently prayed.

Levi was gasping for air. "It's The Dragon, July. If she's not dead, she will kill us. Oh, I hope she is dead." He pranced in place. "July, she had an axe! I can't get killed by an axe!"

"She's not going to kill anyone … at least not right now, Levi. And we'd better hope she isn't dead. It wouldn't be just reform school we would get sent to," July told him.

"We?" Levi was shaking.

"Yes, *we*. Celie, you and I. We're all in this shed on this property. And she didn't even see me. She saw you setting in that auto. I think you scared her to death," July told him.

Levi doubled up and groaned. "We got to get out of here before someone finds us, July."

"Levi, we have got to go for help. We can't leave her here to die." July grabbed his shoulders and looked him square in the eyes.

Levi shook his head. "But that's The Dragon!"

From above Celie answered, "Levi, July is right. We ... we ... we can't let The Dragon die. You know that." Celie was as white as Grams's kitchen curtains. Slowly she got up and crossed to the ladder. "Please, Levi, come make sure I ... I ... I won't fall."

The Dragon moaned.

Celie didn't wait for Levi to come help her. She slid down the ladder, ran to hide behind July, and peeked over her shoulder.

"Maxworth?"

July looked at Levi.

Levi shrugged. "I don't know who Maxworth is."

Celie stuttered. "I ... I ... I think Mama said that was the name of Mrs. Drunyon's husband. Maxworth M. Drunyon. Remember, Levi?"

"That's right," Levi snapped his fingers and whispered.

"Do you think she thought you were her dead husband sitting in that auto?" July asked.

"And that's why she died?" Levi grabbed his stomach again and wailed.

July rolled her eyes. "She is not dead, Levi. She made noise. Dead people don't make noise."

Celie grabbed July's arm. "Some dead people do—ghosts make eerie sounds."

July shook Celie's hand away. "She's not a ghost. She's not dead. And we've got to get her some help. Now!"

"You get her help. Celie and I are going home, ain't we Celie?" Levi hopped over the body and out the door.

"No," Celie declared. "I ... I ... I will not leave July alone. We were in this together, and mostly it is your fault because you made that stupid butter bet with July. She didn't know how much you like butter, so one could say you cheated her. You're being a coward, Levi. I ... I ... I won't be a coward with you."

July loved her cousin Celie at that moment.

Levi threw his head back and turned around. "Okay, you win. But if The Dragon kills us all, or worse yet, gets us all sent to reform school, it won't be my fault. Remember, I wanted to get out of here."

The Dragon groaned once more. Celie pressed herself against the wall of the shed. Levi slipped further away as July dropped to the ground in the shadows of the shed.

The Dragon's eyes fluttered open, but she didn't focus on the kids. She lifted herself on one arm and stared at the Model-T. "Oh, my heart." She grabbed the cloth of her blouse over her chest and twisted it in her fist. "Maxworth. I'm sorry, Maxworth. It was all my fault ... all my fault." She whispered and sunk to the earth again.

"Someone has to stay with The Dragon while I go get help." Levi shouted over his shoulder, and he was gone.

Celie edged out of the building and ran after him. "I ... I ... I'll go get Gramps. He's a pastor, so he'll know what to do. Maybe he can even save The Dragon's soul."

July dumped her head into her hands. "Great, I guess I'll stay with The Dragon." Quickly she tipped her head upward and mouthed the words, "Sorry, God," as she inched away. Mrs. Drunyon's body was too close for comfort.

10

From the Dead

MRS. Drunyon lay still as death. Her skin was an ashen gray. July watched the veins that popped out in her neck to see if there was any movement. July couldn't see any at all. Mrs. Drunyon was close enough July could reach out and feel her veins. She hesitated. Even if the woman's heart was not working, what could July do anyway? She remembered that when little Sydney at the orphanage had almost drowned, someone had pushed on her chest to get her heart started again. July thought this might save Mrs. Drunyon's life, and God would probably expect her to do that. She forced her shaky hand to lightly touch the woman's neck. It was moist and cold, but she couldn't feel a beat. She would have to press harder. She pushed and felt something, but it might have been her own heart slugging away in her chest.

July jumped as the ground thundered with Gramps's pounding steps. Celie trailed behind. July guessed he wasn't as old as she thought a grandpa should be because he sure ran fast. He dropped beside the woman while looking directly at July. His eyes held so many questions that July knew when *later* came, she was going to be in trouble.

Gramps picked up Mrs. Drunyon's wrist and felt for her pulse. "Good. She's got one." July felt relief rush over her. Again Gramps looked July smack dab in the eye. "What happened here?"

Before July could answer, Levi plowed onto the scene with someone who must be his mama. July could see that was where Celie and Levi got their red hair. Yet, her hair wasn't splattered all over the place as theirs always seemed to be. Each strand was in order and didn't dare move. She was the most beautiful woman July had ever seen. July looked at Celie and smiled. Someday Celie would look exactly like her mama. She would be beautiful, too.

Levi's mama stopped for a moment, letting her eyes scan the scene. She didn't seem to be interested in the crumpled woman on the ground. Levi's mama settled her eyes on July as she looked the girl up and down. "So this must be June's girl?"

"Yes, Sybil," Gramps said. "This is June's girl. She has a name you know. It's July."

Sybil sniffed. "June always said she was going to have a July. Is this the only child she had, or are there more?"

Gramps cut in. "Sybil, what we need right now is Doc Hickory, not family talk. This woman is ill. How about you being useful and going to get him?"

Sybil raised her eyebrows. "Really, Ezra, the doctor will be here. I sent Luther to get him. He took the auto to speed things up, so if he's in, he should be here shortly. I know Ida Belle is due anytime now, and she lives five miles out. If the doctor is tending to her, we will just have to wait."

"Let's pray it is not Ida Belle's time, then." Gramps continued to hold Mrs. Drunyon's wrist. The woman moaned. July wanted to laugh as Aunt Sybil stepped abruptly away from the figure on the ground, and Gramps dropped Mrs. Drunyon's hand as if it were a hot coal. That lady even put the fear of God into adults.

"I expect you had best pray over her, Ezra. She doesn't seem very well." Sybil clutched her throat in despair.

"That is one of your better ideas, Sybil." Gramps began to pray. "Dear Lord ... God ... Heavenly Father, please be with this woman."

With relief, everyone heard the auto pull through the alley and lurch to a stop. The door slammed while dust from the road still pillowed over the vehicle. "This way, Doc," said the twins' daddy. "Levi said she was in the shed."

"The shed?" Doc Hickory asked. "I thought it was locked up. She have a key?"

"She must. The door's open." Levi's daddy answered as he ran into view.

July looked at the axe stuck in the wall where The Dragon had thrown it. "Some key," she mumbled.

Relieved, Gramps moved out of the way for the doc, who was pulling his suspenders in place with one hand and carrying his black bag with the other as he trotted across the dry grass. He stepped beside the woman on the ground, knelt down and listened carefully to her heart. He nodded as he leaned in closer. He reached out and felt the veins in her neck, seeking for a heartbeat. July could see the Doc ticking time with her pulse.

Everyone was watching his face when The Dragon surged to life. She swiped his hands from her throat and grasped them in a death grip. "You can't strangle me, Maxworth! You can't come back from the dead and strangle me!"

The doc yanked her boney hands from his and almost fell backwards trying to get away. "Oh, my soul!" he cried and began feeling for his own pulse.

The twins' mama hid behind their daddy, and the two kids were latched onto one of Gramps's legs. July flattened herself against the shed wall beneath the axe—about as far away as she could get without jumping over the woman.

Wildly, Mrs. Drunyon sat up and stared at the doc. She dragged up her hand and pointed a knobby finger at him as she snarled, "Maxworth, get back into your precious Model-T and drive yourself to your resting place, and don't ever come out to bother me again."

Doc swiped his handkerchief over his forehead before he started talking to his patient. "Ma'am."

"Don't come any closer, Maxworth," The Dragon spat.

"Believe me, Ma'am, I won't get a smidgeon closer, but I'm not Maxworth. I'm Dr. Ike Hickory, and I'm here to help you." The doc spoke as soothingly as he could.

"You can call yourself what you want to, Maxworth, but I've known you for too long. I knew you would try this, but it won't work on me, Maxworth." Her eyes remained fixed on the doctor.

July saw the doc motion to Gramps as he continued talking to Mrs. Drunyon. "Ma'am, you've had quite a shock. We need to get you inside where you can rest."

Mrs. Drunyon chuckled. "You would like that, wouldn't you, Maxworth? Me resting while you do what? No, I think it would be best for you to crawl right back into that precious Model-T of yours and cruise to your own place … unless … unless you want to tell me what you did with the bank money?" Her speech had slowed and her piercing eyes glowed with the idea. "Yes, Maxworth, you could tell me about the bank money and where that 'safe place' is that you talked about. I'd like to hear of it. After all, where you live now, money's no good, is it, Maxworth?"

All the while, Gramps and Uncle Luther had been slipping carefully around Mrs. Drunyon. Now, with a slight nod from Doc Hickory, they grabbed her from behind. She squealed and flayed her arms frantically. Dust rose like smoke as she tried to grab something for a weapon. But her grip took July's arm instead. Her glazed eyes settled on the girl. "You?" she hissed. "I should have known you would have something to do with this. You and Maxworth are in this together, aren't you?"

July yanked to free her arm, but it remained sealed in the woman's clutches. As Celie dashed over to help July, The Dragon grabbed Celie's ankle with her other claw. Celie screamed and danced on the sod, trying to loosen the grip.

The doc took this opportunity to shove a needle he had filled with serum into Mrs. Drunyon's shoulder. She gasped. "You, Maxworth? What have you done?" Her speech slurred, and her eyes began to droop, but her clutches still held tight.

July pried the fingers from her arm and knelt to do the same for Celie's ankle. Still Celie danced.

"Quit it, Celie. I'm trying to help you," July ordered.

When the last finger lost its hold, Celie ran crying into her mama's arms. July wished she had a mama to run to. Her heart ached, and she touched the spot Mama's wedding ring fell. It was gone! Slowly, her hand went to her mouth, and her eyes welled up with tears. The ring was gone. Mama's ring was gone.

She looked to where Celie clung to her mama. July heard her Aunt Sybil say, "Young lady, I want you to stay away from that cousin of yours, if she really *is* your cousin. Her mama was no good, and I can tell July isn't worth a plugged nickel either."

Celie gasped as she watched July flinch. She mouthed the words, "I'm sorry, July."

July dropped her gaze. Mama's ring was gone, and now Celie had been taken away. Her shoulders slumped.

Gramps and Uncle Luther were helping Doc Hickory with Mrs. Drunyon. "Well, Doc?" asked Gramps.

Doc Hickory shook his head. "Pastor, I hope I never have a house call like this again. That woman calling me, Maxworth!" He shivered. "Pastor, wasn't Maxworth her husband's name?"

Sandra Waggoner

"I believe it was," Gramps answered.

"Pastor, something awful must have happened to this woman to push her over the edge this way." He whistled, "I hope whatever it was never happens to me."

"I don't guess any one of us wants that," Gramps said as he studied July.

July was in trouble again because Gramps was not going to let this rest. She looked across to where Levi had moved by his daddy. She could tell he was begging her not to breathe a word of what had happened. Well, the bet was done. She didn't owe him a thing, and if she was going to be in trouble with Gramps, Levi was for sure going to be there with her. Again, she touched the empty place close to her heart. Levi owed her big time. Her mama's ring had to be in this shed, and that was Levi's fault. That had been a stupid butter bet. Levi could help her find Mama's ring. It would have to be after everyone else was gone, but if he wanted her silence, he was going to pay for it right here in this dusty shed.

11

Dust Cookies

THE thick, black cloud of dust whined and moaned through the house. It was like a deadly disease sifting under doors and silting through window casings. Even though it was hot, July shivered. She had helped Grams find almost every piece of linen the house could offer and dip it in water. They had wrung it out and pushed it against any dust seepage they found. July hated the second story of her mansion house during this dust storm. If it had felt like ghosts visited before the storm, it now felt like the ghosts resided in corners, closets, and for sure the attic. The ghost choir screeched and clapped thunder drums against the sides of the house. Dry tree branches scratched the wooden slats, and tumbleweeds targeted the house like a mass of volleyballs.

Grams sat in her rocker with her Bible spread over her lap. She wasn't reading, though; she was rocking and watching the walls.

Gramps wasn't home. Before the storm hit, Sam Bryan, the lawyer had come by asking Gramps to accompany him to the sheriff's office because they needed him to make a statement about the Mrs. Drunyon incident. When they left, Gramps had not been very happy, but neither had the skies. Even then, the horizon held a restless aura, signaling something was coming. Everyone hoped for rain, yet everyone dreaded the dry, shifting dust which was most likely to come.

Grams hoped and prayed that Gramps was still at the sheriff's office safely tucked away from this dust storm. Several times July heard the creak of Grams's rocking chair as she said, "These wicked storms can kill a body. Gramps needs to stay put. July and I will be fine. We'll make do. Yes, these wicked storms can kill a body."

July believed her. She went to the window and pulled the curtain away from the pane. There was nothing but thick dust heaving and swirling. She couldn't even see the cedar hedge on the side of the house. There was no way Gramps would be home before the storm settled. She, too, hoped he would stay at the sheriff's office.

"How long will it last?" July asked as she dropped the curtain.

Still rocking, Grams said, "Don't rightly know, July. Sometimes they come and go quick like, and sometimes they last for days."

"Days?" July mumbled. She didn't know if she could make it days shut up in the house like this. She sure couldn't go upstairs and sleep by herself. Outside, the weather was in horrible revolt.

"I'll tell you what, July," Grams closed her Bible. "Let's get cozy in the kitchen and make us some dust cookies."

"What are dust cookies?" July asked.

Grams chuckled. "Why, they are any kind of cookie one would make during a dust storm 'cause I reckon dust is going to be the main ingredient."

July giggled. Actually, she liked the taste of dust. When it hit her tongue, it tasted like the first aroma of rain. Nothing smelled better than rain, especially in this dry land.

Banging dishes in the kitchen was a whole bunch better than rocking and waiting out the storm. Grams tossed some things into her crock bowl and handed the same ingredients to July for her bowl. July couldn't see that Grams was measuring much. It was a handful of this and a pinch of that. Grams used a wooden spoon to mix the thick dough, but when July tried, it just wadded up on the spoon. Finally, she tossed her spoon to the side and dove into the dough with both hands.

Grams shook her head. "Girl, if you ain't a sight. I believe you have sifted flour and dust from the top of your head to the tip of your toes. You may have enough for a dozen cookies powdered over your body."

July laughed. "These are my first cookies ever. I've never made cookies before."

Grams stopped stirring. "Never? You've never made cookies before? Never? Ever?"

"We never had a kitchen," said July. "We had a room and an alley at the end." It was a fact, and that was the way July stated it.

"Oh, July, July. Maybe we had best mix cookies every day for the rest of our days together." Grams began singing, "There's a better day a coming."

July liked her singing and thought a better day had already come. It gave a peace the storm had yanked from her. She tipped her head to the side. Peace was a new experience for her.

"Now, July, you get you a scoop of dough and roll it in your hand like this," Grams showed her. "Then dip the dough ball in this bowl of cinnamon-sugar mix. Make sure plenty of the mix sticks to each cookie. It makes them M'm! M'm! yummy. Then you spread these dough balls over the skillet, and we'll poke them in the oven for a few minutes. You can smell when they're done, and we'll pull them out."

"You wait until you smell them?" July asked.

Grams laughed. "One gets used to the 'done' smell." She opened the oven door and shoved the cast iron skillet into the yawning oven. "When we pull this skillet out, we'll slap your skillet in."

July sniffed the air. After a few minutes, along with the dust, she smelled an aroma which must have had fingers that dug all the way to her stomach. She licked her lips. She had already tasted the dough several times, and it was good. These cookies were going to be super.

"Yep, take a big whiff. Another minute or two and they'll be ready to take out of the oven." Grams smiled.

A dreamy look washed over July's face. "Grams, I think this is better than the smell of fresh rain."

"Cookies and rain," said Grams. "Yes, cookies make a house smell homey, and rain makes a land the same."

As she thought about what Grams had said, July drew with her fingertip in the flour on the table top. Until now, she had never lived in a house or had a home, and she had never felt homey. Grams was homey, so why did her mama leave? Why had Mama traded all this for an alley? July didn't think she ever would make that trade. She looked at Grams. Could she ask her? Would Grams tell her the answer? Did Grams know the answer?

"July, get you a plate off the sideboard, and we'll put these cookies on it." Grams opened the oven, letting heat burst into the kitchen. The best smell ever overcame the dust and wafted through the air. Grams wrapped a towel about her hand, took the skillet handle, and sat it on the table. "If you'll be careful, I'll let you get that spatula and put these cookies on the plate. Now, don't touch the pan because it's hot, and it will burn."

July's mouth watered.

Grams winked. "We'll let them cool a bit and then have us some warm cookies and milk."

July couldn't wait. Grams let July slide her pan of cookies in the oven while she stood close by. Grams even showed her how to wrap the towel about her hand and pull the hot pan out of the oven.

"M'm! M'm! yummy." Grams chuckled, and July agreed completely.

After July had downed two cookies and a mug of milk, she studied Grams. She looked to the plate of cookies and back at her grandma before she asked, "Grams, why did my mama leave this homey home?"

Grams slowly sat her glass of milk on the table and brushed a hand through her hair. "Child, I don't rightly know. She never did say. She was here one day and gone the next." Grams paused before she continued. "She did leave a note tucked in my Bible next to one of my favorite scriptures. I guess she knew I would find it there sooner or later." Grams looked into the distance, but July thought she was really looking into the past. Grams began quoting, "The Lord bless thee, and keep thee: The Lord make his face to shine upon thee, and be gracious unto thee: The Lord lift up his countenance upon thee, and give thee peace." Gram smiled. "I used those scriptures as my prayer for your mama."

July propped her chin in her hands. "Grams, it didn't work." Tears ran down her cheeks. "The Lord didn't bless us and keep us and make his face to shine upon us."

"I'm sorry, honey. Grams is so sorry." Grams spread her arms wide inviting her granddaughter in. July crawled upon her lap. She was ten years old. She really didn't fit in Grams's lap very well, but this was where she wanted to be, and she knew Grams wanted her there.

"Grams, why didn't he shine on us?" July whispered.

"Oh, honey, sometimes you have to look for the S-O-N shine. If the Lord is in your heart, he calls himself your heavenly father. As your father, he can't bless you if you are disobeying him. Honey, your mama shouldn't have run away. We would have taken care of her no matter what. We loved her, and we would have seen her through anything." Grams stroked July's hair.

"You mean my mama running away was disobeying God?" July asked.

Grams nodded. "Did you feel the sunshine with your mama?"

July shook her head. "Not very much."

Grams ran her finger down the side of July's cheek. "I'm pretty sure the Lord would have wanted your mama to stay with us. Our place is a hundred times better than a room or an alley."

"But, God didn't smile on me either, and I didn't run away."

Grams thought before she answered. "July, always know that the things we choose affect those we love. Your mama's choice broke mine and Gramps's hearts. Her choice decided where you would live and how you would live. I don't think her choice made her very happy, either." Grams took July's face and held it in her hands as she looked into her eyes. "July, it is so important to check with the Lord before we make choices."

"But, Grams, I don't feel very special."

"July, you are so special. God smiled on Gramps and me when he brought you here. It's the best God smile we have had in a long, long time." Grams kissed her on her forehead.

July wiped her eyes and looked at Grams. "Then I guess you and Gramps are my first God smile."

Grams hugged her so tight she thought she forgot how to breathe.

12

The Cedar Hideout

J ULY pulled the crumpled note from her pocket and read it again. She didn't have to. She had read it so many times she knew it by heart. "Under the big cedar in the tree row between our houses. Sunday afternoon at 3 o'clock. Celie and Levi. Don't let anyone see you!"

Levi had picked a time after church when Aunt Sybil was busy talking. He had shoved the note in her pocket and hissed, "Later." July had searched out Celie in the crowd, and she nodded her head the minute their eyes met.

"Later." Well, this was later. She didn't have to wonder about the part, "Don't let anyone see you." That had been simple. Grams and Gramps were both napping away. How they did it in those cane rockers, July would never figure out, but sure as shooting, they were both asleep to the world.

She looked at the tall tree. Cedars smelled good, but she remembered the tree outside The Dragon's shed. Celie had been right. It was a prickly tree, and the sap was gooey. July wondered why they had picked a cedar tree for their meeting—other than it was a mighty big one, and she would be able to tell it from the rest of the trees. She'd probably have to climb again.

Sandra Waggoner

She checked over her shoulder and all around. No one was watching. She might as well get this over with. She didn't know what Levi and Celie wanted, but she knew what she had to say. Levi was going to look into Mrs. Drunyon's shed with her to find her mama's ring.

At the edge of the tree, she stopped to see if anyone was in sight. She could see no one. The tree branches brushed the ground, so she dipped to her knees and crawled beneath the branches. A soft carpet of cedar needles covered the ground. July was in awe. It was like a cave under there. The trunk was in the middle, and as the lower branches had grown, they had made a natural hollow all around the trunk as their heavy foliage forced the ends of the branches to sweep the ground all around the tree. It was quiet and secluded. No one could see in. July smiled as she settled against the huge trunk. What a great place for secret meetings. This was just right for a hideout. A tiny bird fluttered through the branches. July thought it was a sparrow. Another bird joined the sparrow, and July knew this was a place she wanted to come again and again, with or without Levi and Celie. She breathed in the cedar smell and relaxed.

A door slammed. "I'll race you, Celie." That had to be Levi.

"That's not fair, Levi. You jumped from the porch," said Celie. "You had a head start."

Levi dove under the tree. "I won." He held the branch long enough for Celie to start under and then let it swing back and hit her in the face.

"Levi, you did that on purpose!" Celie rubbed her face.

"Prove it," Levi said.

"She doesn't have to prove it." July came to her rescue. "I saw the whole thing. You did it on purpose."

"That's because you're a girl. Girls stick together no matter what," he said.

July raised her eyebrows and decided to ignore him. "Celie, are you alright?"

Celie was still rubbing her cheek. "Yes, but no thanks to Levi."

July pulled the note from her pocket. "Good idea about the note. This is one of the best places in Plevna, Kansas. Hey, I haven't seen you for a while. I know there was the dust storm, but that was three days ago. Where have you been?"

Celie looked at Levi before she answered. "We have a problem."

"No, we don't, Celie," Levi butted in. "We don't have the problem. Mama has the problem. She says you're getting us into too much trouble, so we're not to see you anymore."

"Trouble? What trouble?" July asked.

Levi shrugged. "You know. The deal with The Dragon's shed. The police called Daddy down to the station and questioned him."

July narrowed her eyes. "You did tell your mama why we were in the shed in the first place? Didn't you?"

"She didn't ask, so what she doesn't know won't hurt her," Levi said. "Besides, do you know just how much trouble we could be in?"

July thought back over that day. It was the dust storm, and Grams had shown her how to make cookies. Gramps hadn't said much when he got home. He had enjoyed the milk and cookies, and when Grams had asked about the meeting, Gramps warned: "Best leave sleeping dogs lie."

July wasn't sure what that had meant, but she figured she wouldn't ask Gramps any questions.

"What was said?" July asked Levi.

Levi sobered. "They talked about breaking and entering being a crime where reform school might be something to consider."

"Us?" Celie whispered. "Reform school?"

"Celie, Daddy talked them out of it for us since it was our first offence," Levi said. "But Gramps had to do a bunch of talking for July."

"Why me?" July asked.

"The Dragon said you were always in trouble at the orphanage, and you had stolen things before you came. They had a big list of police reports that came with you to the orphanage. In fact, The Dragon said you had more reports when you showed up than clothes."

July glared. "I took a blanket from a clothesline because Mama was freezing, and I took food out of the garbage dumpsters to eat. Mama was sick, and that was the only way I could feed us. If you call that stealing, then I'm a thief. I'm proud of it. I did what I could do to save Mama."

Celie's eyes were huge, but Levi was the one who answered. "The dumpster? You ate food from the dumpster? That's sick."

"Maybe so, but I'm alive," she dropped her eyes. "It didn't help Mama much. She didn't make it."

Celie scooted close to July and slipped her arm in hers. "I'm sorry."

Levi looked up the tree trunk and back again. "Me, too. I'm sorry, but it don't change how Mama feels. I know her, and she ain't going to let Celie and me hang around you."

"Yeah, she calls you 'alley trash,' " Celie added.

July shrugged, "I guess that's what I am. *Alley trash.*"

Celie squeezed July's hand. "I don't care about trouble. You're the best cousin I could ever have, and I'm sticking with you. We can meet right here under this tree, and Mama will never know."

Levi was more practical. "Go ahead, Celie. I'm not letting July get me into any more trouble. There's no way I'm going to reform school."

July started thinking about what Levi said. "Me? I got *you* trouble? Did you tell your mama we went into The Dragon's shed because of *your* butter bet?"

Levi dropped his eyes to the ground.

"No, he didn't tell her about the bet," said Celie. "And he didn't tell her he sat in the Model-T—and that The Dragon thought he was her 'Maxworth.' He didn't tell her anything about that."

"So your mama thinks it's all my fault?" July couldn't believe it.

"And she thinks you're alley trash," Celie added.

"I have news for your mama. I don't live in an alley anymore, so I can't be alley trash," July frowned.

"I know that. I don't think you're alley trash, but Mama does. That's why we have a problem. I like you, and you make a great cousin," Celie told her. "We thought you might have an idea about what we could do to change Mama's mind."

"I do. Levi could tell the truth for once. Then your mama wouldn't think it was my fault. Then she might like me." July stared at Levi.

"That ain't happening. I'd be in hot water like you wouldn't believe," said Levi.

July shoved her face close to his. "It is going to happen ... unless you go back to that shed with me."

Levi backed away. "I ain't going to that shed again, and you can't make me."

"Yes, you will." July gritted her teeth.

Levi shook his head. "You can't make me."

Celie giggled. "He thinks the shed is haunted."

"You do, too," Levi glared.

Celie nodded. "Yes, but you were the one who said you felt 'Maxworth' tickle your neck when you were sitting in the Model-T."

He glanced at July to see what she thought.

"It was probably a cobweb," July laughed. She knew that would make Levi mad, and she was glad.

"No, it wasn't. And I heard him whisper, 'This is my Model-T. If you don't get out, I will take you to my place,' real quiet like. It was more scary than The Dragon, and she was plenty scary." Levi wiped sweat from his brow.

July pulled her knees up and rested her chin on them. She steadied her eyes on Levi. "Even if Maxworth's ghost is in that shed, you and I are going in there. I lost something important, and we have to find it."

"What could be that important?" Levi asked.

There was no way July wanted him to know it was her mama's wedding ring. It was too personal, so she told him it was a necklace from her mama.

Celie softly spoke. "Oh, that makes it so special. I'll come help look for it."

"I'll bet you'll help her. Did you listen, Celie? IT IS IN THE DRAGON'S SHED: THE HAUNTED SHED."

Celie gave a wide-eyed nod. "I know, Levi. I know, but this is July. I'm going to help her find her mama's necklace."

"Well, you two have fun because I'm not coming. I never want to go near that place again, and you can't make me." Levi started to crawl out from beneath the cedar.

July grabbed his foot. "Yes, I can."

Levi stopped and turned. "How?"

"So help me, if you won't come, I'll march right to your front door, and I will pound on it until your mama answers, and I will tell her it was all because of you we went into Mrs. Drunyon's shed in the first place."

"She won't believe you," Levi smiled.

"Then I will tell Gramps," July said.

"So? Gramps don't like to cross Mama, either." Levi was enjoying this.

"Then I'll go to the police. I'll bet they would like to know all the facts." July crossed her arms.

Levi sighed and dropped his face into his hands. "Okay. When do we go?"

July formed her lips in a grim line. "Now."

"Now?" Levi squealed in grief.

July spread her hands. "Gramps and Grams are asleep, and I guess your mama and daddy are, too. So, we don't have to worry about them seeing us together."

"July's got a point, Levi," said Celie. "I'm for getting this over with. I vote with July on this one."

"Girls always stick together," Levi groaned. "Fine. We'll meet in ten minutes."

"Where?" July asked.

"Under the sign on the corner," said Levi.

July looked him in the eye. "How do I know you'll show up?"

"Cross my heart and hope to die." Levi made an "X" over his heart.

"You had better believe you will die if you don't show, but I have a better idea. If you don't show, you have to go to the cemetery and sleep the whole night on Maxworth's grave," July said.

Levi gulped. "I can't do that."

"Then you had better be there." July spit on her hand and held it to Levi.

Levi was so worried he didn't even notice the spit until he had shook. He glared and slid it down the side of his pants.

Together they stacked their hands one on top of the other and promised "on Maxworth's grave" that they would meet, go inside the haunted shed, and find July's necklace. If one of them didn't show, that one would have to spend the night sleeping on top of the grave.

They decided to leave the tree one by one from different directions. Levi would go one way around the block and Celie would go the other. July would cut through the vacant lot on the back side of The Dragon's place. They would meet under the street signs for South Laurel and Hazel at the end of the block in fifteen minutes sharp.

The Ghost of Maxworth

JULY stood beneath the sign on the corner of South Laurel and Hazel Streets. She was the first to get there, and she wasn't holding her breath waiting on Levi and Celie. They had better come. At least Levi had better come. July brushed her fingers through her hair. He owed it to her, and his future depended on him keeping his word.

Levi snuck up behind July and grabbed her.

"Ahhh!" she yelled.

Celie ran from down the street and kicked him in the leg.

Levi yowled. "Why did you go and do that?"

Celie held her hands on her hips. "Why did you scare July?"

"That's my business," Levi glared.

"Levi, answer me."

Levi was the first to drop his eyes. "I thought maybe I would see if The Dragon would wake up."

All three turned toward the back door of The Dragon's house and waited. When nothing happened, July raised her eyebrows. "Thank you, Levi. Your plan worked. No Dragon."

Levi turned and spat in the dry grass.

"You were hoping she would catch us before we could get into that shed, weren't you?" July asked.

"So what if I was? It's a creepy place. I know you don't believe me, but Maxworth is in there. Somehow, someway, Maxworth is in there," Levi said.

"So, you believe in ghosts?" July asked.

Levi shook his head. "I didn't think I did."

"Good," said July. "Let's head that way."

"But after I sat in his Model-T and felt him and heard him? I don't know ..."

"Forget it and come on," said July.

"Do you want to go through the door?" Celie asked. "It isn't chained up anymore."

July pressed her lips together. "I think we have to retrace our steps. That means we climb the cedar and go through the window. Maybe my necklace got caught on one of the branches of the tree."

"I hope so. Then we won't have to go in that haunted shed." Celie wiped her brow.

"I'm all for that," Levi said under his breath.

July was glad for the hot afternoon sun, yet it still was shadowy in the cedar. Slowly she climbed up, but not without checking each branch. She would be glad, too, if the necklace had been caught here instead of somewhere in the shed. "You both look on all the branches in case I missed seeing my necklace," she told them.

By the time July had climbed to the window, her hope was dwindling. It would have been so nice to have found it before they had to climb into the dusky shed. "Any luck?" she asked.

Celie answered for both. "Nothing."

With a sigh, July crawled through the window into the loft of the shed. She waited for Celie and Levi to join her. The shed was shrouded with stillness, and uninvited slivers of sunlight filtered through the slats of the roof. Because the dust lay so thick, their tracks from a few days before were easy to follow.

July broke the silence with a whisper. "Let's get this over with."

Levi's eyes were wide. "You feel him, too, don't you?"

Celie shivered. "I do."

"Levi," July warned, "keep your trap shut."

She stepped forward, and Celie grabbed the edge of her dress. "Don't leave me."

July turned to soothe Celie and gloated at Levi, who had a tight grip on the back of Celie's dress. "Calm down, Celie. I'm not going to leave you, but don't forget to be looking for the necklace."

Slowly, they crossed the rafters and found nothing. At the top of the ladder, July stopped. Maybe it had gotten caught on the rungs, but she couldn't see anything. The light was dim in this corner. They would have to go down to the bottom level of the shed. She turned and stepped on the top rung. Halfway down the ladder she looked up. Levi and Celie both were white as sheets.

It took every bit of courage for Levi to talk. "We'll wait for you here."

"No, you won't, Levi. A deal is a deal. If I have to go down, you have to go down. Now come on."

When July planted her feet on the solid ground floor, she was relieved to find Celie and Levi following. She looked at the Model-T. How close had she been to it? She couldn't remember, but she knew she had been by the auto's door. That was just before The Dragon had bashed the shed door open, and July had plastered herself against the wall and slid in the dirt. Chances are that was where she had lost the necklace. It may have caught somehow on the wood, so she headed for the door. "I think this might be the best place to look," she told Levi and Celie.

Neither said a word. July watched them steer clear of the Model-T. Really, they were not helping her look, but at least she wasn't in this shed alone.

July brushed her hands along the wall she had smashed herself against trying to get away from The Dragon. She followed it to the ground and searched over the floor. She found nothing. Her heart was busting. She sat back along the wall and rested, wondering where else it might be. This was the place she noticed it gone. It had to be in here somewhere.

Levi and Celie sat beside her and snuggled close. Levi was the first to break the silence. "Okay, we looked. We didn't find nothin', so I say we get out of this creepy shed."

"Just a minute," July paused. "We could pray."

Levi squinted his eyes in disbelief. "July, even I know you can't ask God to help you do something that is in the middle of doing something you are not supposed to be doing."

"What?" July asked.

Levi hissed. "We're not supposed to be in here. It's breaking and entering. How can you ask God to be with you when you're doing that?"

July sighed and leaned back against the splintery wood. "I don't care. I need God's help."

"Dear God," she whispered, "it would mean a bunch to me if you would let me find Mama's ring."

"You didn't close your eyes," Levi accused.

Celie jabbed him in the side. "You don't have to close your eyes to pray. Don't you remember the picture in the family Bible? Jesus is looking up into Heaven while he is praying."

"That works for Jesus, not regular people," Levi said.

Levi and Celie continued to argue. July shut them out. She looked at the dancing particles in the sun streams. The light slipped into the roof and tried to shine in the dreary shed. July gazed at the Model-T. She felt her heart start pounding. She stood up and crossed to the automobile.

Levi jumped and ran to her side. He grabbed her hand and swung her around to face him before she could reach the shiny black beneath the layers of dust. "You don't want to touch that Model-T. Maxworth's spirit is in it! Believe me; I know. I heard him, and I felt him!" Levi was frantic.

July was in a daze as she pointed back toward the Model-T. "But look, Levi," was all she said.

From the windshield wiper the frayed shoelace ran like a straight road on a roadmap over the top of the glass and dangled above the steering wheel. Her mama's ring danced, catching the light and sparkling as it swung.

Levi slapped his hand over his mouth then yanked it away. "You were never in that auto. Maxworth must have hung it there. It must be a trick to get you inside. Maxworth must want your soul." Levi was shaking.

July stepped toward the Model-T. "Don't be silly. I want my mama's ring. I'm not even going to get in the auto. I'm just going to reach in and grab it."

Like a streak, Celie ran and smashed between July and the automobile. "No, July. Levi says Maxworth's spirit is in there. Don't even think of it."

"Celie, it's my mama's ring. I didn't risk my neck just to leave her ring in that Model-T." July pressed her to the side.

Levi took her arm to hold her back. "July, Maxworth's ghost is in there. You can't take a chance of making him mad."

"Listen, Levi and Celie, you heard me. I prayed to God just a minute ago, and I believe God found Mama's ring for me. It would be like a slap in the face of God to leave it there because you think some sort of ghost is here. I'm telling you right now, God has got to be stronger than any ghost."

Levi and Celie were shaking, but they gave in and slid to the side.

July clasped the handle of the door and pulled. It screeched as it opened, sending chills up and down her spine. July reached up and yanked the shoelace from the roof of the auto.

Just outside the old shed, a sing-song voice broke into the air. "Maxworth, I hear you in there."

"Oh ... oh ... oh!" Celie began her dance. July grabbed her and dragged her toward the ladder. Levi flew by and was half way up the ladder before the girls could even reach it.

July pushed Celie up and over the top of the ladder and dove after her just as the door opened. The Dragon stepped into the doorway and stood for a moment, letting the sunlight silhouette her body.

"Oh ... oh ... oh," Celie whispered.

Levi slapped his hand over her mouth, and July held her finger to her lips, motioning for them to be quiet.

"I heard that." Slowly, The Dragon advanced into the *haunted* shed. She stopped and listened.

The three in the loft held their breath.

The Dragon swiveled her neck, scanning the shed. She stopped, and a smile came across her lips.

"Maxworth, you have been here again. You left the door open to your precious Model-T." The Dragon gently walked to the auto. She got inside and swung her legs into driving position. "Maxworth, I would very much like for you to tell me where you hid our treasures. I have searched everywhere I can think of, and I've come up empty-handed." She took hold of the steering wheel. "Please, Maxworth, I could use the money. They took my job at the orphanage, so I guess I will have to stay here in this horrid, little town. And one of those orphanage brats took our wedding ring, but I will get it back."

By now Celie was biting her fingers, and Levi's knuckles were white. July was trying to keep her heart from racing.

The Dragon continued in a soothing voice. "Maxworth, I'm going to give you a chance to think about this. I know you always liked to think on things before you made big decisions. I will mosey into the kitchen and make us a spot of tea. I'll wait for you there, but don't take too long. I get rather impatient at my age." The Dragon slid from the automobile, softly shut the door, patted the side of the Model-T and walked to the opening in the shed. Before she left, she turned and blew a kiss toward the auto.

It was so quiet in the shed that the three heard her crunch across the grass, clomp up the steps, and go into the house, closing the door behind her. No one talked for a while.

In the rafters, July pressed her hand to her chest trying to slow her heart. The shoelace strung through her fingers dangled and danced with each beat.

Finally, July broke the silence. "She's gone. I think we're safe."

"That was creepy," Celie whispered.

Levi glared at his sister. "The Dragon is crazy."

July placed her trembling hand over her heart. "I am so glad I prayed!"

Levi shook his head. "I told you, you can't pray to God when you're doing something wrong."

Celie shrugged. "July can't pray anyway."

July tipped her head to the side. "Why?"

Levi glared at Celie in warning.

July repeated. "Why can't I pray? I did pray, and it helped a bunch."

"Mama said you can't belong to God. He doesn't take in people like you."

July dropped her mouth open. "I suppose she thinks that because she calls me alley trash?"

Levi gritted his teeth. "Celie, you can't keep your big mouth shut, can you?"

July was wild. "So, she thinks alley trash doesn't mean a thing to God? Right?"

Celie spread her hands. "It's not just the alley trash stuff. It is mainly because your mama was never married, so you are one of 'those kind' of people God doesn't forgive."

"Ah ha! Your mama is wrong. My mama was married, and I have this to prove it." July pushed her mama's wedding ring in front of the both of them. "This is my mama's wedding ring, so there. This proves she was married. You can go home and tell Aunt Sybil that God does take people like me even if I used to be alley trash." July stood up and stomped across the loft to the window.

Levi stopped her. "Your mama was not married."

"Yes, she was. I have her ring." July dangled the ring in front of them.

"July, what is your name?" Levi asked.

She glared, "You know my name. It's June July Calendar."

"What was your mama's name?" Levi asked.

July was becoming more and more frustrated. "You know it. It was May June Calendar."

Levi took a fast breath. "And what is Grams's name?"

July dropped her shoulders. "Come on Levi, I just know her as May Calendar—Grams."

"Think about it," said Levi. "May Calendar, May June Calendar and June July Calendar."

"So?"

"All the last names are the same: Calendar, Calendar and Calendar. That means your mama never got married. Her name never changed. You don't have a father," Levi spoke quietly.

July mouthed the names over, "Calendar, Calendar, Calendar." She threw her hand over her mouth, "Oh, Mama wasn't married, was she?"

Celie crossed to July. "That's why God won't take you. Your mama never married, so you are one of 'those kind' of people."

July dropped her hands to her side, the ring dangling from her fingers. She mumbled, "God doesn't want me?"

Celie touched her arm. "But we want you."

"God doesn't want me?" July turned and ran to the window. She dove into the cedar and climbed down, swinging from one footing to another. Branches slapped her, but she didn't care. She slid to the ground, scrambled to her feet and wildly ran.

"Wait, July, wait!" Behind her she felt Levi's pounding footfalls, but he would never catch her. She would make sure of it.

Celie was yelling over and over, "But we want you, July!"

The Lie

JULY stampeded up the porch steps and threw open the door so hard it hit the wall.

Grams came running. "July? What is wrong?"

July's roving eyes sparked. "Where is Gramps?"

"He went to the church," Grams said. "What has happened?"

"He lied to me! Gramps lied to me!" Tears of anger traveled down her cheeks, and she didn't even know it.

"What? Honey, Gramps does not lie." But before Grams could cross to the little girl, July had stormed back out the door and ran blindly across the yard.

Levi blocked her way and tried to stop her. With a force of anger, she smashed him to the side and barreled around him.

Levi scrambled to his feet and flew after his cousin. "Wait, July!" he yelled, struggling to catch his breath.

Her path led her straight to the church. She flew up the steps and shoved the double doors open to the sanctuary. She faced Gramps at the other end of the aisle.

Gramps was startled. "July?"

Every inch of her body was tight with rage. She choked out the words, and as they came, they grew in fury. "You lied to me!" Her hands were in knots. "You lied to me!" She pounded his chest with her fist.

Gramps's voice remained steady. "July, I don't lie. The truth comes hard sometimes, but I don't lie. I learned that lesson years ago. Best you sit a spell and settle down. Then we can have a little talk."

July shook her head violently and spat out the words. "I won't sit in this place. It belongs to God, and you and I both know God doesn't want me here."

"Whoa, whoa, little girl." Gramps held his hands in the air, but he hesitated to come toward her. She was like a frightened deer that would run at the first sign of movement. "Just what makes you think God doesn't want you here?"

"This." July yanked the shoelace holding her mama's wedding ring and held it high in the air. "This is not a real wedding ring. Mama wasn't married, and you knew it, didn't you? Still, you told me God wanted me and there would be a place for me in Heaven. Well, you can have the ring, and you can have God, and you can have Heaven! You can have all of it!" July threw the ring at Gramps.

Only an instant passed in silence as the ring clanked on the wooden floor. Gramps stooped to pick it up. "July, who have you been talking to?" Gramps asked.

A storm thundered up the church steps and trampled into the meeting house. Levi was first. Celie's was next. She had a death grip on her mama's hand and was dragging her through the double doors.

"Ezra, I want you to keep that piece of alley trash away from my children." Aunt Sybil's face was red, and her eyes sparked with anger.

July swirled to meet Aunt Sybil. Her hands on her hips, she was ready to fight. "I am not alley trash, and I don't want to hear it anymore."

Grams was winded as she rushed through the doors. "Ezra ..." She stopped and looked about as if she were trying to figure out what she had just walked into.

Gramps strolled down the aisle and sat on the arm of a pew. "I think we're about to have a family 'come-to-Jesus' meeting. Sybil, set yourself down. Levi, Celie and July, have a seat in front of Sybil. May, close the doors and sit close to them for me, please. Don't let anyone in."

"You can't keep us here," Sybil sputtered.

Gramps ignored her. "Sybil, is that son of mine at work? If he isn't, we need him here, too."

"Yes, Luther is at the depot on duty," she clipped her words.

"Then we will have our meeting without him. Sybil, you can tell him about it later, or better yet, have Luther come talk to me," Gramps told her. "Everyone, sit down."

Everyone sat but July.

Gramps motioned to a place on the pew. "July, we are waiting on you."

July's every muscle was tight. "I can stand. I already told you I know God doesn't want me here, so I would rather not sit. And I really don't want Aunt Sybil behind me."

"July, I am your grandfather. You live with me, and you will do as I ask. That is how it works. Now, have a seat. If you prefer, you may sit across the aisle from your Aunt Sybil."

July clamped her lips together and glared toward Aunt Sybil. She did live with Gramps, and she had no other place to go. God might not want her, but she was pretty sure Grams and Gramps did. She turned into the pew across the aisle and flopped down on the wooden seat. She crossed her arms and waited.

Gramps began, "No one leaves this church house until this is settled. First off, who told you that God doesn't want you, July?"

July would not let a word budge from her lips.

Levi burst out, "It was big-mouth Celie. That's who did it."

Gramps's clear blue eyes settled on the little red-haired girl. July thought her frazzled hair sprang out even more with fear.

Celie swallowed. "I wish I didn't do it." She turned to July. "I'm really, really sorry, July. I didn't mean to hurt you."

Gramps interrupted. "Thank you, Celie, for your honesty. Now, can you tell me why you told July that God doesn't want her?"

Celie turned to look at her mama. Her voice trembled. "Mama."

"Mama told us July couldn't go to Heaven because God didn't accept her kind," Levi added.

Gramps took a deep breath as he focused his eyes on Levi. "And what 'kind' is July?"

Levi sucked in, "I can't say that word," he glanced at his mama.

Quietly Gramps asked, "Why not, Levi?"

Levi sat up straight. "Because," he wailed, "I'll get my mouth washed out with soap."

Aunt Sybil jumped into the conversation. "That is one of the reasons I don't want my kids around her." She pointed at July. "They don't need help learning bad words."

Gramps held his hand up to silence Aunt Sybil. "Levi, who said this word that you cannot repeat?"

Levi's eyes popped wide.

"Go on, son, who said the word? Was it July?"

Levi shook his head.

"Then who have you heard use this word?" Gramps asked.

Levi scooted to the front edge of the pew. "Mama," he said quietly. Then he ducked his head before his mama could thump him.

"Sybil?" Gramps asked, "What is her 'kind'?"

"You know, Ezra. You're the preacher. You read your Bible, so you know what type she is."

"I guess you will have to tell me, Sybil," Gramps said.

Sybil pursed her lips together. "Her mother was not married to her father. You know what that makes her." Aunt Sybil was seething. "I cannot have her kind around my children."

Gramps's face was hard, and July thought he was pushing Aunt Sybil into a tight corner which she could not get out of. "Sybil, I guess you have talked this over with your husband?"

Aunt Sybil dropped her head and studied the floor.

Gramps continued, "That is what I thought. Now, I want everyone to listen to what God says in his Good Book about her 'kind.' In the book of Joshua, God tells us about Rahab the harlot, and I'm sure it is a term you do not want your children using either, Sybil. July, you are not to use it, either, but you need to know what it is, and that God loves harlots as much as anyone else he has put on the face of the earth. Joshua was instructed to save her and all who would come into her house when the Children of Israel took the city of Jericho. It was because she had kept the spies safe from her own people, choosing God above her own. In the book of Matthew, Rahab is named in the lineage of Jesus Christ himself. So, I am figuring God loves harlots, too."

Gramps paused to let that soak in and then continued. "Again, in the book of John, Jesus tells about the woman who came to the well to fetch water. Jesus told her he had water, living water, that she might drink of and never thirst again. When this woman asked for the water, Jesus answered in such a strange way. He told her to go get her husband. That was her problem—her sin. She didn't even have to tell Jesus what was wrong. He told her. 'Thou hast well said, I have no husband: For thou hast had five husbands; and he whom thou now hast is not thy husband.' Do you think this woman with five husbands and living with a man, drank from the well of living water? You bet your boots she did. Sybil, this very woman at the well could be your next door neighbor in Heaven someday, if Heaven is where you are going," Gramps said seriously.

Aunt Sybil gasped, "How dare you ..."

Gramps stopped her. "It is a startling thought, Sybil."

"But ..." Aunt Sybil began.

"I am not finished," Gramps interrupted. "Whom does God love? Levi and Celie should know the answer to that question." Gramps turned his blue eyes to them. "Quote John 3:16."

Levi began, and Celie joined in. "For God so loved the world, that he gave his only begotten Son, that whosoever believeth in him should not perish, but have everlasting life."

Gramps nodded, "Now, Levi, who is 'whosoever'?"

Levi shrugged, "I guess it is anyone who breathes air."

Gramps chuckled. "That is the best way to put it. I like that answer, Levi. Anyone who breathes air, and that only cuts out dead people. Your decision to believe has to be made when you are alive. Now, does anyone who breathes air include Celie?"

Levi and Celie both nodded.

Gramps continued, "Does it include Levi?"

Again, they agreed.

This time Gramps was specific. "Sybil, does that include July?"

Aunt Sybil straightened the skirt of her dress and squared her shoulders before she answered. "I suppose."

Gramps's eyes softened. "July, honey, are you breathing?"

Slowly, July nodded.

"July, honey, does God care for you?"

Again, she agreed with a nod.

"July, honey, God cared so much for you that he gave his only Son to die so you wouldn't have to. Honey, God loves everybody so much, especially you," Gramps ended in a choked whisper and spread his arms wide.

Slowly, July stood up and stepped into the aisle. She stumbled and dove into his arms. It was the best place to be in the whole of Plevna, Kansas. No, the whole world!

Columbus

WHEN Gramps gently pulled away from July, he took her hand and opened it wide. Very lightly he placed her mama's ring in her palm. "July, your mama wanted you to have this ring."

Her eyes swimming, July said, "But Gramps, this ring is a lie. Mama wasn't married."

Gramps took her hand and closed her fingers over the ring. "Did your mama wear this ring?"

July nodded, but never let her eyes leave his.

"Did your mama love you, July?" he asked.

"Yes," she mumbled.

"Then I expect she gave you all she had to give. In her heart, this ring was a commitment between God and her. It may have not been legal, but she did what she could. July, your mama would want you to learn from her mistakes. Can you do that?" Gramps ask.

"I think so," July said.

Gramps patted her hand before he continued. "The biggest thing you can do to show you loved your mama is to forgive her. Now, I know you don't like lies, but can you forgive your mama?"

July blinked and pressed her lips together.

Sandra Waggoner

Gramps pushed a bit further. "July, if you don't forgive her, it won't hurt her. She will never know. But if you don't forgive her, it will hurt you. It will make you bitter. Bitter doesn't taste good, and it sure doesn't feel good. You know if you put bitter vinegar in a can, it will eat right through the container. Bitterness will do the same thing inside of you. It will eat right through your soul, and it will hurt with every single bite it takes. It will eat so many holes in your heart it will be like a sieve. You won't be able to hold a single drop of love for anyone or anything. I want you to think about it. God wants you to forgive your enemies. Your mama was someone you loved, so it should be easier to forgive her. Don't you think you should try?"

July let the tears tumble. She thought she had cried more since she had been with Gramps and Grams than she had in her whole life. Could she do what Gramps was asking her? July swiped her hand across her face. "You mean forget mama lied to me?"

Gramps shrugged. "I suppose God could help you forget in time if he chooses to, but you have to forgive first. There is no way you can forget if you haven't forgiven first."

July's pulse was racing. Deep down she knew Gramps was right. She looked to the rafters holding the roof in place. God was kind of like those rafters. He would hold her in place. A smile played at July's lips. God was a rafter? She turned back to Gramps. "I will try to forgive Mama. I think God will be my rafters."

"What?" Gramps searched her face.

July pointed upwards. "Like the rafters hold the roof on the church, I think God can hold me up while I try to forgive Mama."

Gramps chuckled. "That will preach."

July gave a decided nod. "I forgive Mama." She felt warm love surge through her heart, and it didn't hurt when it beat anymore. Forgiving wasn't hard at all.

106

July is Coming

Gramps leaned in and kissed her forehead. "July, you are the best smile God has sent our way in a long time." He took her hand and unfolded her fingers, picked up the worn shoelace holding her mama's ring and slipped it over her head to drop around her neck. "Remember, your mama loved you no matter what else she did in this world."

July patted the ring in place, then she hugged Gramps's neck tight. When July let go, Gramps stood to his feet. He looked at the family sitting before him. "I think this meeting calls for a celebration. Levi and Celie, I want you to take July to our house and stay there. When your daddy gets off work, he'll make some ice cream. I like ice cream, and this is a hot day. Grams was telling me the cow is giving lots of cream, and we need to use it. Will that help you, May?"

"You bet it will help. I'll go along and get started." Grams turned for the door.

Gramps cleared his throat. "Not yet, May. You let those kids out and close the doors. We adults are not done here."

Grams nodded and headed to her post.

Gramps shooed the kids toward the doors. "Go on with you, and don't get into any trouble."

Levi and Celie jumped up and were delighted to head outdoors, but July was curious. What did he mean by the meeting not being over? Were they going to talk about her? When Grams shut the doors, she tip-toed back and laid her ear against the crack.

Celie saw what she was doing. "July, you can't do that."

"Shhh," July pressed her fingers to her lips.

Levi laughed. "Celie, let her get in trouble. Gramps will apply the hand of knowledge to her seat of learning."

July didn't hear a thing Levi said. She was trying too hard to hear what was happening inside the church. She motioned for Levi and Celie to keep it quiet.

Levi sat on the bottom step. "I want to see how this turns out," he said.

Gramps was talking. "Sybil, we have a problem. You told a hurt, little girl God didn't want her because of something her mama had done. You told Levi and Celie they couldn't play with her."

Sybil stuttered, "But she is making them do things ..."

Gramps stopped her. "Sybil, she cannot make them do a thing. Levi and Celie made their own choices."

"But ..." Sybil tried again to interrupt.

"Sybil, I don't want your two-cents worth. It's time for you to listen. Mostly I leave you alone and let you flounce about with your highfalutin' ways, but not this time. July is our granddaughter, and we are responsible for her. We love her just as much as we love Levi and Celie. So this time, Sybil, you are going to listen to me. Understand?"

July had to strain to hear Aunt Sybil's answer, but she must have agreed because Gramps went on preaching.

"That little girl out there is your children's cousin, your niece. Both Levi and Celie have taken to her, and she thinks the world of them, too. She can't help what her mama did. You ought to know God won't send her to Hell for something her mama did. You owe her ... " Gramps stopped, and July heard him stand to his feet. "May, make sure those kids are not listening at the door. They don't need to hear any of this."

July dove from the doors and down the steps, tripping over Levi. Neither took time to stand. Wildly they crawled around to the side of the church where Celie was hiding. Celie smashed her fingers to her lips, and hissed, "Quiet!"

By now, Levi was doubled over in silent laughter at July's crash landing on top of him.

The doors swung open, and Levi froze.

After a pause Grams said, "All clear, Ezra."

"Hmm, May, why don't you leave the doors open and watch for us. This won't take long, will it Sybil?"

Levi shoved the words through his clenched teeth: "We got to get out of here. Come on." He motioned the girls to follow as he led the way behind the church.

"How did Gramps know someone was listening?" July wondered.

Levi slapped his leg. "He just knows everything."

"He's a preacher, July. God probably told him," Celie added.

July wrinkled her brow. "God does that kind of thing?"

Levi said, "You can ask Gramps how he knew you were listening, July."

July glared at him, but Levi looked so ornery. With that wicked gleam in his eyes, freckles smattered all over his face, and his red hair spewed in every direction, she dropped to the ground in glee. Levi doubled over and fell to the ground alongside July.

Celie didn't understand what was so funny, but she didn't want to be left out. "Hey, what happened?" Celie stomped her foot and caught it on Levi's leg. She stumbled and crashed on top of July and Levi. The pile was alive with laughter.

To their horror, the back door of the church was thrown open, and Gramps stepped out the door. "What in the world …?" He stopped and looped his thumbs through the straps of his overalls. "I see. You got scared away from eavesdropping by the front doors, so you thought you would try listening at the back door?"

Celie sat up fast. "I didn't eavsdrop anywhere."

Gramps raised his eyebrows.

Levi pulled himself from the pile and shoved his hands into his back pockets. "I told July she would get in trouble for listening."

Gramps settled his gaze on July.

She sat with wide eyes. "I quit when Levi told me it was wrong."

Gramps was trying to hide a smile. "And when you heard me tell Grams to check the doors to see if anyone was there?"

July blinked. "Yes, I guess it was after I heard that, too."

Gramps sighed. "You three had best make your way home a sight faster. We will be along shortly, and I'll take care of this mess when I get there."

"Yes, sir." July scrambled to her feet and ran. Levi and Celie were close behind.

When they hit Grams and Gramps's house, they collapsed on the porch, dragging in great gulps of air. All three lay sprawled across the porch boards. Their heads formed a hub, and their bodies spread in a circle like the blades on the top of a windmill. The shade felt good, even if little fingers of sunrays tickled their faces through the leaves of the catalpa tree at the side of the porch.

Levi broke the summer stillness. "Hey, when we were in the family 'come-to- Jesus' meeting, Gramps was doing all the talking. I didn't understand half of what he said. There was no way I was going to interrupt him to ask him anything, but ..." he paused to gain courage. "I'm not sure what that harlot thing is. Do you know?"

Celie answered, "Come on Levi, don't you even listen in school?"

"We studied harlots in school?"

"You studied them in school?" July was all ears.

Celie sighed. "Yes, in history. Everybody studies it in history. Do you remember now, Levi?"

"This is summer, school is over, Celie. I don't even want to try to remember what I learned in history. Just tell me," Levi demanded.

Celie gave in, "The Harlot was the name of one of Columbus's ships when he discovered America."

"Oh," Levi said, "so Columbus's ships are going to be in Heaven? That is weird."

July burst with laughter. "You really believe that, Celie?"

"That's what we learned," she said.

Again July laughed, "I'd like to know what kind of grade you got in history. A harlot is not one of Columbus's ships, Celie."

Celie sat up. "It isn't? Then what is it?"

July sobered as she studied the shadows from the catalpa leaves. "Celie, that is something you will have to ask your mama or maybe Gramps. There is no way I'm telling you what it is. Your mama already doesn't want you around me."

"Come on, July. You know Mama isn't going to tell us. Just whisper what it is, and we'll never tell anyone," Levi begged.

July knew she shouldn't. She studied Levi, but it was Celie she had compassion for. What if Celie forever recited Columbus's ships as the Nina, Pinta and the Harlot? July sighed and gave in. She motioned for them to gather in close. For only their ears to hear, she whispered the disgusting definition.

Levi was wide eyed.

Celie gasped, "That is what it is? Oh, July, I'm sorry." She held her hand to her throat. "Oh ... oh ... oh, July! That's what your mama was?"

July jumped up and glared down at Celie. Her feet were in fighting position and her hands in tight fists. "I wish I had never told you! I wish you had gone to your grave telling everyone a harlot was one of Columbus's ships! Then everyone would know how stupid you are!" July stomped to the door and slammed it behind her. She ran up the stairs and threw herself on her mama's bed. She smothered her head in Mama's pillow. She could forgive her mama, and she could pray God would help her forget. But how many other people knew? There was Celie and Levi and Gramps and Grams and ... Oh, no! There was Aunt Sybil. Aunt Sybil would tell all of Plevna, Kansas—if she hadn't already. Would they forgive her mama? July pounded the sagging mattress with her fists. Would they ever let her forget?

The Taste of Ice Cream

"**JULY**, honey, wake up." Grams brushed the little girl's hair from her forehead.

July dragged her eyes open and slapped them closed again as memory crashed around her. As long as she had been in the dark about Mama not being married, it felt like the whole world around her was, too. Now, everyone would know the shady secret. Maybe the streets were a better place. No one there knew. No one cared where you came from. On the streets people accepted you like you were. Never, ever, did anyone ask about your past. That was your business, and you only talked about it if you wanted to. And if you did say something about your past, people didn't croak over it. Maybe it would be easier than being Aunt Sybil's *alley trash*.

"July, the family is waiting downstairs." Grams rustled into July's thoughts again.

"Go away," July struggled with the words. She knew they would hurt Grams, so she kept her eyes closed. She didn't want to see the hurt in Grams's face. Grams had never done anything bad to July, and she knew she should speak nicer to her grandma.

"No, July." Grams reached over and took July's hand. "It seems I had a conversation like this with your mama. She told me to go away, and that is exactly what I did. Then she went away, and I never saw her again. That carved a crevice in my heart deeper than the Grand Canyon. So, little girl, you had better get used to me because I will not lose you like I lost your mama."

Slowly, July opened her eyes and studied Grams's face. Somewhere from the desolation deep within, July groaned, "But Grams, you know I am Aunt Sybil's alley trash. I can't change that."

"July, you are not alley trash. With God's help, you decide what you are going to be. It is not about what someone else dubs you. Only you can make that decision. Remember what Gramps told you from God's Word? God takes what you are, and with your permission, he makes you into what he wants you to be. You just have to give him the right to do it. July, are you willing to let God make you what he wants you to be?"

July thought. Gramps had said Rahab was a harlot, and God let her be in the lineage of Jesus Christ. Rahab had watched a lot of people get killed, and she probably saw it again and again every time she closed her eyes. Watching people get killed was a whole lot worse than what July's mama had done. Still, it was awfully painful. "Grams, will it hurt forever?"

"Sometimes. Does it hurt now?" Grams was very serious.

July nodded, "Right here in my heart it feels like someone dug a deep hole."

"That is life, July. Sometimes life hurts. God uses time to heal those hurts if you let him. Healing is a blessing that comes from God. When you are what he wants you to be, it is like God spreads frosting on your path. We can look back and see the rough spots in the road, and if you look closely, they are filled with great dollops of frosting. The rough spots are still there, but they get farther and farther away.

It is good to remember the hurt. It helps us to know what to do the next time and how to help others going through just as much pain as we are."

July asked, "You and Gramps, you love me?"

"Oh, yes. More than you will ever know. You are God's smile on us."

July touched mama's quilt. Mama had loved her. July sat up. "You and Gramps make double the love I ever had. Mama loved me. That was one. You love me and Gramps loves me, so that makes two. That is double the love."

Grams scooped the little girl into her arms and hugged her tight. "We had best head downstairs before the rest of the family comes looking for us."

July pulled away from Grams. She had to go be with the family. She felt heavy inside. Every single one of them knew Mama's past and what she was. July knew it had to be done, and it would be the turning point for her. If they would not accept her as family with the past forgiven and forgotten, she would head back to the alleys. She loved her grandparents and refused to be a bother to them. She heard train whistles all the time. She would wait until dark, sneak out the back door, and hop a train to somewhere … anywhere. It didn't matter. All her life she had been sneaking. It might be easier now because she would be taking God with her. She took a deep breath and straightened her hair. She nodded to Grams. "I'm ready, Grams." She wasn't really ready, but if she waited until she was ready, the time would never come.

Grams stood and stretched out her hand, inviting her little granddaughter to join her. "Coming?"

"Yes, ma'am." July rose to her feet and stood as tall as she could stand. "I'm ready to face the music."

Grams smiled, "Now, July, music is from the Lord himself. It can be a very wonderful thing. Let's go."

And it can be a bunch of rumble and roar, too. July didn't share her thoughts to Grams, though. She let Grams go first. Maybe it would be safer that way.

The kitchen was empty, but the makings of ice cream were strung over the table and piled by the wash tub. July could hear the chatter of everyone out on the porch. Grams swung the screen door open and held it for July. Silence settled the instant Grams stepped into the scene. When July crossed the threshold to the porch, everyone stared at her. She could feel a warm, red glow spreading over her cheeks, and she knew everyone noticed. She couldn't think of a single word to utter.

Gramps stopped cranking the ice cream freezer and turned to Celie and Levi's father. "Son, your turn to wear your arm out for a while." He smiled at July. "A nap in the middle of the day? I must be working you too hard, girl."

Celie ran to her side. "July, I hope you like strawberry ice cream. We had wonderful, juicy strawberries in the garden, so I told them it was your favorite."

"I don't know if it's my favorite or not," July said. "I don't even know if I like ice cream. I have never had ice cream before."

"What?" Levi bellowed. "You've never had ice cream, any kind of ice cream? Ever?"

"Nope. They don't serve ice cream in the orphanage … or in the alleys … and ice cream is too hard to steal." July didn't crack a smile.

Levi's eyes were huge as he looked from his daddy to Gramps, and July thought he was waiting for all the trouble to bust open that she was going to be in. She could tell he didn't want to be any part of it.

The quiet that settled over the porch was like the plop of one lone fish in a pool. Ripples spread that didn't dare to make a noise. Yet, when each ripple touched a face of those on the porch, their feelings stirred and then darted beneath a deep, shadowy surface.

July knew what they were thinking. She was unwanted. She was too much trouble. They had better stay away from her and for sure keep the kids away from her. Maybe reform school would be a better idea. All their faces showed those feelings.

Well, tonight she would sneak out, head for the train station and hop a boxcar to ... it didn't matter where. Anywhere would be better than having people look at her like this.

Celie tip-toed over and slipped her arm around July's rigid body. "Now that you are with us, you won't have to steal anymore. I don't care what your mama was, and I don't care what you have done. I still love you, July. You are the best cousin ever."

July couldn't say a word.

Levi slipped over to July. He dropped his arm over her shoulder. "Same goes for me, July. You're the best."

July tried to swallow. Levi thought she was the best? Not one single word could be pushed out without a sludge of tears bursting loose.

Uncle Luther stopped cranking. "Ice cream's done." He was watching somewhere off in the distance, refusing to even look July's way.

Gramps cleared his throat. "I guess we will have to make ice cream a monthly family celebration."

July wanted to shout out that it was not ice cream she wanted. It was being with Celie and Levi. They liked her the way she was, and it didn't matter what her mama had done. Yet, she knew there was no way Aunt Sybil was going to let her cousins be around her. Not after today. Aunt Sybil wasn't even here. And Uncle Luther? He wouldn't even look at her.

"May, get the bowls and the spoons. Let's eat this ice cream." Gramps winked, "July, you've not tasted anything as good as this, so you get the first helping."

Grams came with the dishes and a big spoon to dip ice cream. She removed the towels piled on top of the ice cream freezer and brushed the ice away. Grams pulled the lid off and handed Gramps the long spoon. He dunked it into the strawberry mass and dragged out a heaping spoon load. He dropped it into the bowl and pushed it toward July. "Okay, July, you are the taster. Tell us how it is."

All eyes were on July as she took the bowl. Grams handed her a spoon, and July dipped it into the ice cream. As she started the spoon journey to her mouth, Levi was drooling. Celie's eyes glowed, and she would probably clap if July loved the ice cream.

July thrust the spoon in her mouth and closed her eyes. She couldn't help the little moan of pure wonder. Surely this taste would be in Heaven. Angels must eat ice cream.

Celie danced around her cousin. "It's good isn't it, July?"

July nodded and shoved another bite in her mouth.

Levi slapped her on her back. "My turn." He knelt at the ice cream freezer.

When all had their bowls in hand, peace settled over the porch. July surveyed the scene. She was going to miss this. July noticed Uncle Luther's thoughts seemed to be as far away as his gaze. Finally, he sat back. "There she is," he said.

July looked down the sidewalk. Aunt Sybil's shoes were clip-clipping down the cement. July straightened to get ready for the big blow. Now was the time. Aunt Sybil would be yanking her children away from her bad influence. July dropped her eyes. She knew Celie felt it, too, because she scooted a little closer to her.

Levi asked, "Want some more ice cream, July?"

Aunt Sybil stopped at the steps to the porch.

Gramps spoke, "Sybil, I see you took your own sweet time."

"I was busy," she retorted.

Uncle Luther asked, "Was it where I thought it was, Sybil?"

Levi threw his head back with a moan and whispered, "She found it."

"What?" Celie hissed.

"The spank stick. I hid it. After today when we got caught eavesdropping at the church, I figured it was coming," Levi groaned.

"You hid it?" Celie couldn't believe it.

"Oh well, it was worth a try," said Levi.

Their daddy laughed. "Levi and Celie, I hear very well, but your mama and I were not talking about the spank stick. It is good to know it is not lost, though. Confession is good for the soul, isn't it, Levi?"

Levi rolled his eyes and groaned again.

Celie hit his shoulder. "Just dig the hole deeper for us. Okay, Levi?"

Gramps joined in his son's laughter.

"Actually, I was searching for this." Aunt Sybil took her hand from behind her back and displayed a small wrapped package.

"Is it someone's birthday?" Celie asked.

Aunt Sybil pressed her lips together. "No, your father wanted me to do this. It is a "welcome to our family" present for July."

July was not the only one who gasped. She and everyone on the porch except Aunt Sybil's husband dropped their mouths open.

"Come on, July. Come open this present." Aunt Sybil held it toward July, her eyes not quite meeting the little girl's.

When July hesitated, Uncle Luther nodded. "It's our way of saying we are glad you are here and a part of the family. Go on, July, please."

Slowly, July stood, crossed the porch, and took the gift.

"Come on, July. Open it." Again Celie was clapping and dancing.

The only present July could ever remember getting was the ring her mama had left her. Gently she loosened the white lace ribbon and unfolded the delicate pink flower-splattered paper. It revealed a small box, and when she lifted the lid, her eyes filled with tears.

"July, what is it?" Celie begged.

July reached into the box and pulled out a fine but sturdy gold chain.

Aunt Sybil explained, "It is to hang your mama's ring on. It was an old chain your uncle gave me. It is real gold mind you, but we wanted you to have it. Besides, that string you have is rather filthy. No niece of mine is going to go gallivanting around with a dirty string about her neck."

July held the chain in the air. The sunlight through the catalpa tree made it glitter. "It's beautiful, just beautiful. Thank you, Aunt Sybil."

Aunt Sybil brushed away the thanks. "It is from all of us in the Calendar family. Here, let me put the ring on the chain." Aunt Sybil went to work. She tossed the old string to Levi. "Son, throw this away, and wash your hands."

When Aunt Sybil had the necklace put together, she gruffly ordered, "July, turn around, and I'll put it on for you."

July felt the ring drop into place and patted her precious present. She looked over the porch full of family. There sat Grams hugging Gramps, and both of them were swiping tears. Celie was still dancing, and Levi had taken advantage of the situation. He was scooping a second heaping bowl of ice cream. Uncle Luther had slipped beside Aunt Sybil to put his arm around her and squeeze her shoulder with love. To July this was the best present anyone could give, and the biggest smile God had ever spread on the face of the earth.

July licked her lips and tasted strawberry ice cream. She lingered over the taste. Forever, srawberry ice cream would be the taste of family—the best taste in the world.

In the distance, a train whistle echoed over the little town of Plevna, Kansas. Home. There would be no hopping a train tonight. This was her home now.

July is not having an easy time at her new school, but matters become a lot worse when her teacher is replaced by an old enemy who still wants her mama's ring.

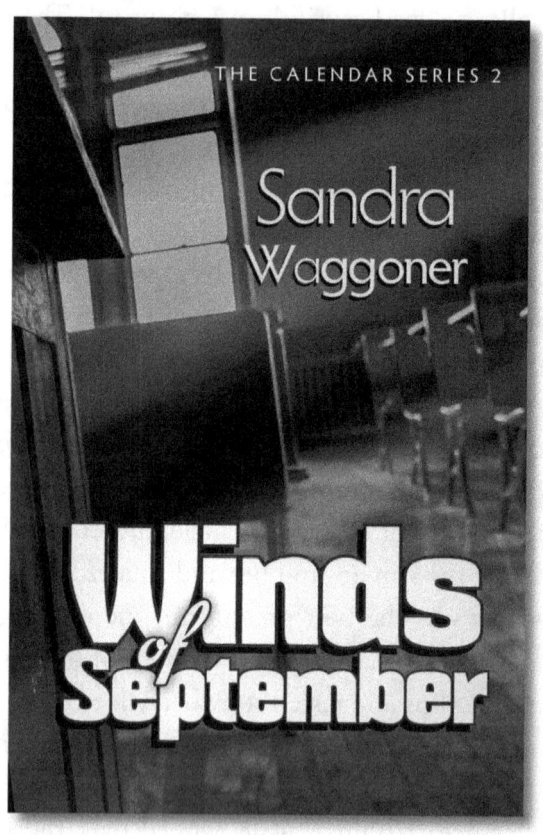

Winds of September

Book 2 of the Calendar Series
Now available!

July's newly discovered grandmother gives her a box of her father's boyhood keepsakes, but it also contains a mystery she has decided she must solve!

Gift of December

Book 3 of the Calendar Series
Now available!

Place your orders at
sablecreekpress.com/bookstore

A secret pain that only love can heal.

Maggie's Treasure

Book 1 of the Gatlin Fields series

Now available!

Only coals of kindness can save Maggie now.

In the Shadow of the Enemy

Book 2 of the Gatlin Fields series

Now available!

Dustin determines to avenge his mother's death even if his father is a coward.

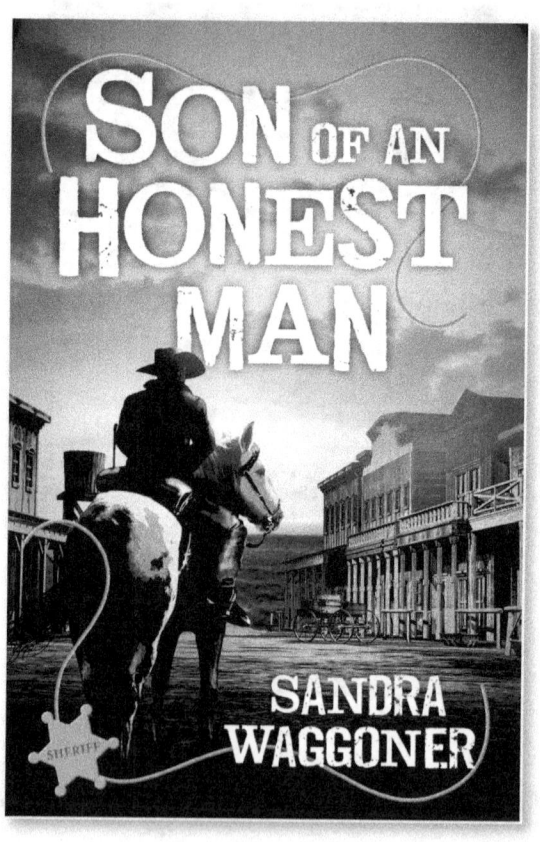

SON OF AN HONEST MAN

Now Available!

A DANGEROUS MISSION.
A DEADLY WOLF.
A DETERMINED YOUNG MAN.

DANGER AT WOLF ROCK

Now available!

Place your orders at
sablecreekpress.com/bookstore

www.ingramcontent.com/pod-product-compliance
Lightning Source LLC
Chambersburg PA
CBHW072005170626
46813CB00005B/2022